TWISTED TALES 2022

DIFFERENT PERSPECTIVES

Edited By Xena-Jo Draper

First published in Great Britain in 2022 by:

Young Writers
Remus House
Coltsfoot Drive
Peterborough
PE2 9BF
Telephone: 01733 890066
Website: www.youngwriters.co.uk

Printed and bound in the UK by BookPrintingUK
Website: www.bookprintinguk.com
YB0514H

Lucy Arbuckle 174
Finley Marchant (13) 175
Indy Turpin (12) 176

Torlands Academy, St Thomas

K Fierce (15) 177

Truro & Penwith College, Truro

Michael Stafford 178
Maddy Vincent (17) 179

Upton Court Grammar School, Slough

Siddhartha Sharma Adhikari (11) 180

Westholme School, Blackburn

Anayah Quddous (12) 181
Elizabeth Judah (12) 182
Jack Valentine (12) 183
Sanad Saidan (14) 184
Esa Iqbal (12) 185
Zaeemah Ali (14) 186
Olivia Ko (13) 187
Jacob Cronshaw (11) 188
Amaan Iqbal (14) 189
Farhan Dudhiya (12) 190
Ismael Karolia (12) 191
Francesca Iles (14) 192
Sophie Holt (12) 193
Harry Gallery (13) 194
Maia Lewis (13) 195
A.Akitha Silva (11) 196
Annabelle Waller (13) 197

Wickford Alternative Provision, Wickford

Sonny Buckley (13) 198

Wingfield Academy, Rotherham

Sofia Spisakova (12) 199

Workington Academy, Workington

Sophie Irving (12) 200
Kobie Metherell (13) 201
Lexi Williamson (13) 202
Reece Sowerby (12) 203
Olivia Conyers (12) 204
Hollie Gallacher (13) 205
Cameron-John Allison (13) 206
Hayden Turpin (12) 207
Madison Robinson (13) 208
Holly Bennett (13) 209
Scarlett Olvanhill (12) 210
Neve Stephens (13) 211
Jaydan Knowles (13) 212
Jacob Allison (12) 213
Scarlett Edmondson (13) 214
Bailey Musgrave (13) 215
Jamie Stoddart (13) 216
Nathan Mallinson (13) 217
Abigail Bewley (13) 218
Aaron Moore (12) 219

THE
STORIES

THE END OF THE END?

All it took was one laceration to the neck. The End has taken too many lives of those who can't rest peacefully, their charred reincarnations swarming the soldier. What was left of its shell-like armour revealed a feeble man who by now struggled to lift his weapon. A faceless silhouette, disparaged and vulnerable, glanced up at the warrior, staring at him in Inertia. The entire realm began to quake as his shadow stood upon the headless ghoul. The shell's debris reformed on him. It was burning his skin, covering him like rain, leaking into his memories, repossessing its power.

Daniel Alzir (13)
Ackworth School, Ackworth

THE REVENGE OF MICKEY MOUSE

I still haven't forgotten when those wretched mice stole my life's purpose by making little kids who used to be happy to come to Disneyland, now fear my presence and crawl into their parent's arms. But I had a plan. I visited my old hunting ground, Disneyland, and went to the basement of the castle to visit my mice friends and terminate them. I succeeded. They reverted me back to my former self and I rejoined my former success as Disneyland's mascot for life and kids were rejoiced to see me, but I wasn't reverted to my former ways.

Ocean Isherwood-Martin (13)
Ackworth School, Ackworth

RECOGNITION

Who am I? I cannot tolerate her overshadowing me anymore. I must win. This is the only way. I lurk through the ventilation system. No one mourns. Forgotten. Unimportant. No one cares and no one ever will.

On the outside was perfection. Anyone who saw her would stare in awe. I was never looked at twice. Boys only approached me to request dates with her. Why not me? At home, she'd torture me. One day I decided to paint her an even prettier picture: covered in mahogany.

I'll tell you who I am. I'm your demise. My reign begins.

Olivia Dyson (12)
Ackworth School, Ackworth

THE RISE OF THE DARK SIDE, I THOUGHT

They say I betrayed the Jedi Force. Temptation transfused through my body, urging me to destroy the Jedi. Internal hatred, death, souls, fighting. They took my life, made me train to fight in a war that I didn't want to fight.

"I shall not be led, I shall be the one to lead." As the successor of the Dark Side, my aim was to destroy the Jedi. As I was looking out at the gloss black abyss, all the hatred, death and fighting left my body.

My son's a Jedi... I finally realised what I did: I made a mistake.

Finn Wood (12)
Ackworth School, Ackworth

KAI, BACK FOR REVENGE

I was defeated by the dragon warrior, Po. That panda shall not beat me again. I trained in the Spirit Realm until I was as strong as the Furious Five and Po put together. I left the Spirit Realm and sought the panda village. Once I found the village, I hauled myself up the mountain and saw Po. I used my weapons, crafted by the gods themselves, to absorb his life force to make myself stronger and completely annihilated the panda village. It was a bloodbath, panda after panda falling, then the Furious Five came. They're gone.

Adam Gill (12)
Ackworth School, Ackworth

MY WARNING TO YOU ALL

I'm evil. Yes, I know I am. Only I know who hides behind this wall I put up, this mask I hide behind. Only I know the truth. Beneath it all, I'm just this 'misunderstood soul'. No. You've got it all wrong, everybody has. Now they are going to face the consequences, everybody is. All it takes is for me to snap my fingers and the world is my oyster. I'll play you all like a puppet, me as the strings master, and you just follow my orders. I'm not just any fairy in the moors anymore, I'm Maleficent.

Mayah Bristow (13)
Ackworth School, Ackworth

RESTORATIONS OF THE HEART

It's funny how something so beautiful can be taken so quickly. My captivating green skin being torn apart into a combustible crimson antagonist. My heart had been stolen from the one I trusted, and I was out to seek revenge. Maui, Shapeshifter Of The Night, and a petite girl. The audacity they had to come back here. He stole from me once, but never again. What was that? It shone like my past beauty. It was my heart. It was one day to be returned. She was the chosen one. The heart of Te Fiti was restored, TeKā was gone.

Olivia Hillas (13)
Ackworth School, Ackworth

MINA 0%

I am Mina 53%, the percentage sign indicates how many people I've killed. I'm going to make it 54%. I'm going to kill Mickey Mouse. He killed my family, I'm getting revenge. He was at a hotel, in his room. I saw him and instantly thought of death. As I walked to the room I felt nervous throughout my body but I didn't hold back. When I was at the door, it was open. I got in. I saw him. I walked closer, pulled my gun out and shot. It wasn't Mickey Mouse. I turned around and he was there.

William Glossop (13)
Ackworth School, Ackworth

MIMICKED

I've done it. I've found the perfect place for my deeds. A wonderful forest, so empty, yet full of life. A place where people get lost, but nothing bad happens here. It's a trusting place. I can blend in when it's dark. Nobody notices my siren head, or lanky arms and legs. They're too busy trying to find someone who doesn't exist. I, simply, mimic who they love. I lure them in and then rip them apart. Eat them. *Devour them.*

Mila Peszko-Keniger (13)
Ackworth School, Ackworth

HORRIBLE HALLOWEEN

I never really belonged on Earth but it only feels normal to kill. Every day I find new victims that are either bad people or are relatives of bad people. As I arrived at their house, I found out that no one was home so I decided to drown their home in petrol so when they got home they would burn down slowly until they turned into ashes. When they got home, inside I hid in the basement and lit the petrol. I ran out and I locked them into a dressing room...

Ashton Coulson (13)
Ackworth School, Ackworth

A NEW WORLD

Dea was living her never-ending life as a fourteen-year-old popular teen. She didn't miss her dad, but her dad missed her. In his room, around a dimly lit candle, Death was chanting an incantation.

"Tick back time, tock back clocks, bring me one who will never have a life clock!" Death continues, "Past planets, over plains, return her to her greatest name!"

And then, a figure formed, Dea. "Father?! ...Why?! Bring me back to Earth!"

"Dea..."

Dea's hatred spread and Death became the evil villain you know and hate.

"You will pay! All of you, and your evil ways!"

Mia Blabolil (12)
ACS International School, Cobham

REVENGE AT LAST

Finally, I'm just about to win. That puny teen is kneeling down in agony. This is it, this is the time to execute him after he killed... her. I draw my bow, the shiny crimson arrow aiming at his head. "Time for you to pay your debts," I say. I shoot the arrow, but it doesn't do a thing at all. It simply just bounces off his head. I look at him in awe, he has this orange glow in his eyes. He gets up, hips squared and throws a hard punch at my chest. How did I lose? How...?

Ranbir Singh (12)
ACS International School, Cobham

GREED

He struck once again, grabbing our food with careless greed. Today, I would get my revenge. Last lesson. Baking chocolate chip cookies. Or rabbit dropping cookies in his case!

The tram rattled and rumbled. He sat there, stuffing his face, and smacking his lips, crumbs raining down his uniform. Of course, such a greedy boy would have to finish every single cookie, wouldn't he? He didn't have room for any more stolen ones.

I gave a secret smile. It took all my willpower not to laugh out loud. Tramping about on that rain-soaked field yesterday was worth it after all!

Harry Boardman (12)
Bury CE High School, Haslam Brow

THE EVIL QUEEN

So, you think you know the story of me, the Evil Queen? Ascended to the throne, became a diabolical witch, and poisoned the princess. What drove me to this, you ask? Let me tell you. Ever since my husband died, there was a piece of my soul missing.

Suddenly, the mirror materialised, mesmerising. But it hoaxed me into using witchcraft and made me a puppet in its game. Driving me to insanity and lunacy, making me think my beloved Snow was trying to overthrow me, it manipulated me into poisoning Snow and roped me to my doom.

Mia De Sousa
Bury CE High School, Haslam Brow

MANSION MURDER

One day, Belle was exploring the forest when she came across a massive mansion. Nobody had seen this before and she wanted to investigate further. She wore a flabbergasted expression as objects communicated with her. In fear, she saw a huge shadow on the wall. A beast approached her, she anticipated growling, but he spoke calmly and gently. Afterwards, they went on a leisurely stroll. Soon she had gained his trust. One day, they went into the kitchen but only one of them left, with a big furry coat.

Olivia Gilkinson (11)
Bury CE High School, Haslam Brow

SPLAT

Splat. The blood slowly trickled off the knife landing on the floor. *Splat. Splat.* The body draped across the bed. It was quite a shame; the bedding was pretty. But now a red puddle stained the pretty white flowers. *Splat. Splat. Splat.* Wind coming from a fan across the room made the temperature drop. A shiver, but not coming from the body lying on the bed. It deserved its fate. But the grey carpet nor the bedding didn't deserve to get dirty in the process. They were simply silent witnesses to the rightful fate. The knife kept dripping. *Splat.*

Marta Closa Cervera (16)
Cirencester College, Cirencester

LOVE FOR FEAR

I used to be weak. I was weak until the world created something better. The world created something, which I gained my strength from. But there's always a price. For some, it's the abandonment of hope. Others, belief or happiness. Mine was love. I used to love freely but that made me weak. So I traded being loved for something better. Being feared. Do I regret my decision? Sometimes. But where's fun in being loved when being feared is so much more useful? What's the point in needing a mortal's heart when having a mortal's fear gains you immortal power?

Madeline Hope-MacLellan
Clayesmore School, Iwerne Minster

FEAR ALWAYS REMAINS

The towering, black structures that surround us will forever echo those screams. Those pitiful cries, never to be answered but soon to leave a silence to deafen any soul, a cold reminder of their failures. The moon looms above, illuminating my acts below as if positioned to be my own personal spotlight. Centre stage in witness for my... victories. And yet my favourite part still is watching the fear fill their eyes as the blood evacuates their pale skin, leaving what remaining life they may have left to fade away into nothing.

Will O'Hara (15)
Darwen Aldridge Community Academy, Darwen

IF ONLY

Why does life hate me? I just wanted people to know who I am and say, "Wow look at Hunter, he is so nice, he saved his sister!"

But that will never happen, I've already been caught and I am about to be sentenced to death, and she will never recover.

My sister got deadly ill, and I had to find some money to save her, but I might not be able to anymore.

If only Jake did not catch me, if only Sylvia was not on the verge of dying, if only my parents didn't die on an exhibition.

Ayisha Shabbir (14)
Essa Academy, Bolton

REVENGE

"Make one wrong move and I'll blow your damn head off!" the vigilante snarled.

"Who are you?" the hero questioned.

"You really have no idea do you?" Slowly lowering her hood to reveal a young girl, her eyes flamed with rage and deep scars across her face.

"No, I watched him kill you."

"Don't you dare lie to me! I trusted you and you just left me to die!" she screamed. "You always told me to focus on what I want to achieve and it'll happen. Well, do you know what I want now? I want you dead!"

Evie Holloway (18)
Exhall Grange School, Ash Green

VILLAIN

Another few innocents dead because of the never-ending turmoil society is in. If only the past wasn't what made this Hell. Now I am back in prison. It's the same old story, the same old loop. Good conquers evil. Prison acts more like an inconvenience than a correctional facility. There they think of these fancy words to say what I am or what I have. But you can't define me. The psychiatrists try to console me but they don't know the past. I guess it's back to the old plan. Another breakout, another escape, another newspaper. People are ignorant.

Ralph Watkins (11)
Gravesend Grammar School, Gravesend

THE WEATHER TEMPERER

The weather. It's coming. What do I do? The relentless storm has a conscience. It knows who it's targeting and that is me. Its creator. Yes, I made a thing that can destroy worlds in a matter of days! It can reduce matter to dust, and I created it. This world is about to die. I can no longer run away. I have to fight. I leap inside the beast, aiming for its core and I start to flail as I hit nothing except a wall of air. I get battered, beaten, pulverised and cut. My body goes limp, nothing.

Guy Partridge
Gravesend Grammar School, Gravesend

FATE OF THE DEAD

Finally, I am slowly succeeding in capturing and torturing the enemies of my granddaughter. The formula is ninety percent complete. I am almost capable of resurrecting my family from the dead. Together, we can haunt and curse the plague upon this earth, the humans. My plan is in motion. The final ingredient needed for my recipe is the blood of my precious great-grandchild, as he is the only surviving member of my family. Subsequently, I need to find their bodies for the ritual to proceed. But I must continue to assassinate whoever enters my territory. My most cherished method, decapitation.

Shayaan Mughal (12)
Heritage Academy, Birmingham

THE REVENGE OF MR WILSON

It was time to activate Undercover Mode. I crept across the shadowy street submerged in trepidation. I had to dash to the rear window which was ajar. My spider senses revealed to me that the neighbour was still around. I felt unsettled. I'd seen him sleep before then but soon turned back towards creeping towards the basement. I lifted my crowbar out of my briefcase and started to detach the first plank of the basement door. Just as I was about to eradicate the other plank, the neighbour lifted the detached plank from behind me and hammered me down, mercilessly...

Eesa Ibn Asif (14)
Heritage Academy, Birmingham

THE MONSTROUS NIGHTMARE

I was once haunted by a monster who imprisoned me in a dark, black underground cell mercilessly and whipped me for no apparent reason. I'd wondered why for a long time, and now I finally might get to know.

All of a sudden a figure appeared in front of me and my soul tightened. Surprisingly, he was frightened of me and started reversing backwards. I looked at my arms then at him. It appeared we had switched bodies. I used all of my capability and broke the impenetrable, aluminium cage. Now everyone will soon face my ultimate divine wrath!

Ibrahim Eslam (12)
Heritage Academy, Birmingham

THE VILLAINOUS HERO

I still have not forgotten the day that I, the hero of New York, betrayed everyone I knew for my own survival. Such a rancorous plot it was. It all started when I was approached by someone I will never forget, someone who tore my whole life apart. I was compelled to let off a poisonous gas in the city and in return, I kept my life which I wish I had relinquished. I hid for many years and was not found guilty, but it was when I made my appearance that I knew I had made a big mistake.

Muhammad Eslam (13)
Heritage Academy, Birmingham

TWISTED THOUGHTS

I was floating away from my body as I saw myself being stabbed until the blade went through the end of the mattress. There wasn't any blood on the sheets, only on the knife and the wound in my stomach. I could see my face and I have never seen anything like it before; I couldn't recognise myself. I was pale, my mouth was wide open and my eyes were almost popping out of their sockets. I was traumatised. I then realised I was never stabbed, it was my inner thoughts, drowning me as I tried to sleep every night.

Melissa Grant (14)
Holbrook Academy, Holbrook

I DIDN'T WANT TO DIE

I didn't want to die. Dying is the reason I did all I did. Despite knowing I would be seen as the epitome of evil. And now the Horcruxes are destroyed and I am doomed. I stare into Harry's eyes. All the effort, the big army I built, all the people I killed, was all for nothing. Everyone knows me as Voldemort. The darkest wizard of all time, but what they really don't know is that I didn't want to be evil. I just wanted to be wanted.

Morgan Rudge (15)
Holbrook Academy, Holbrook

THE RELUCTANT REAPER

Sitting on a throne, I felt a tug on a string tying me to all animals and I knew immediately someone needed greeting into the Afterlife. Floating down from my home in the sky, I got to where I was needed, and I saw a family with tear-stained faces in a hospital looking at an old, frail man in a bed. I knew he was the one I was here to collect. I watched his eyes slowly close, and he sighed. His soul floated up from his body and I took him as my own even through my own unwillingness.

E L
Hospital Education Service, Coventry

WORLDWIDE

I arrived in the UK around the 31st of December 2019 and over the last three years, I've managed to infect almost everyone in the world. I never meant to but after some scientists accidentally left open the door to my petri dish, I couldn't resist a world tour! I really didn't mean to hurt anyone but I'm so contagious and when I then met this amazing girl, Omicron, well... We've shared an incredible life together but now there's a vaccine. And although it will soon end our lives, I'm glad we can't hurt anyone anymore.

Bella Hawkins (13)
Hurst Lodge School, Yateley

THE END OF MANKIND

That superhero act was all a lie. As the sun went down I got to work. At last! My evil invention was finished! It moved from its position and started moving around. I told it its instruction. To destroy all mankind! It obeyed and stomped out of the house. I heard screams of people and house explosions. My plan had worked! I walked out and breathed new air almost. It was amazing! Only villain world! The boss would be very happy. The cold breeze almost felt good. Well, now it did. The apocalypse of death to mankind would be successful!

Freya Hall
Kepier Academy, Houghton-Le-Spring

THE EVIL CAR

Finally, I was about to sink my jagged teeth into another car. Every night when my owner is asleep, I race down to the junkyard. Tonight, was no different. But as I pulled up, I spotted the police and my owner.

"Why was he here?" I cursed. I was just about to have my dinner in peace. I stopped my engine and listened from the shadows.

"There's a half-dead body in this munched up lorry!" exclaimed the policeman. I couldn't listen anymore.

"I only did this to protect you!" My lights shone on my owner's petrified face.

M R
Kingsley School Bideford, Bideford

THE HORRIBLE WITCH

I still haven't forgotten the way my parents treated me!
They would yell at me for getting terrible grades at school,
but they didn't understand. How was I meant to concentrate
at school when everyone throws paper at me and trips me
over? My name is actually Rosie, but people call me the
horrible witch. I'm only horrible to people who are horrible
to me. If you are nasty to me, I will turn you into a frog. I am
a nice person with a soft heart. I hate casting spells, but
sometimes I get so angry and *poof!*

N O

Kingsley School Bideford, Bideford

THE SPIDER GIRL

I still haven't forgotten my childhood. Hi, I'm Spider-Girl and I love spiders. If you are wondering what I mean about my childhood, then listen up! When I was little, the class would always make fun of me for loving spiders. It made me feel so sad and angry. So, this is what I did. And anyway, what is wrong with spiders? They are great! The person who made fun of me the most was Mark. Well, let's just say he's been taken care of. Now no one makes fun of me, I make fun of them! *Haha!*

M B

Kingsley School Bideford, Bideford

THE NOISES

I could hear unforgettable noises. Noises that would stay in my mind for a long time. It was like I was in a horror film. As if there was a fearsome monster watching over me. It went on, day after day, non-stop, but I couldn't find out was it was. Until one day the noises were extremely loud, which I couldn't ignore. I looked into the mirror, and there it was, an enormous creature menacing over my shoulder. That's when I found out what it was, not something you would find in your day-to-day life, but Death.

Nauman Hafeez (14)
Kip McGrath Education Centre, Burton-On-Trent

ANIMATRONIC TAKEOVER

How it started... I was walking to school and I met my friend Jack who wanted me to visit an old junkyard instead. I said, "No thanks" as I had heard sinister things about that place. Jack replied, "But you can find lots of different robot parts there."

So we went and met the old man who runs the yard. He said, "I will give you an animatronic endoskeleton for free..." We took it home and I fell asleep.

When I awoke, I felt weird and looked down at my metal hands and thought, *now I need to get Jack...*

Connor Larkin (16)
Lakewood School, Bangor

STRIKE

The building rises above me, filled with untroubled, carefree families eating dinner. It makes me sick. I take the final match and light it slowly, relishing in the power that comes with holding such a destructive force. I watch as the lethal flame burns its way to my fingers, practically hearing it screaming, "Drop me, let me do what you really lit me for." As my inner fuse runs short, a malevolent smile rises to my face. I release a baleful laugh and let it go. One final hysterical scream emerges before everything goes red. I go down grinning.

Rebecca Bloor (15)
Loughborough Amherst School, Loughborough

METAMORPHOSIS

Restlessly awaiting the salon sunbeds, fantasies of the result engulfed her. UV lights whirred, she implored them to grace her with a beautiful, darker, 'normal' complexion. Bitter nostalgia for her childhood arose. Relentless days of school children labelling her as 'ghastly', or 'corpse-like'. Finally, she could be... normal. It grew to become uncomfortably humid, but she assumed this was normal. Warmth? No, inexorable heat. Puddles of sweat formed by her feet. She convulsed in her cocoon. Her eyes examined for the nearest exit; they met the sign above. 'Test Room 3'. Violet rays embroidered burns upon her skin.
This. Wasn't. Normal.

Taha Mamsa (16)
Manor High School, Oadby

DEATH AWAITS!

"Argh!" screamed Tiffany, who had just been crowned princess a few days ago. Her scream woke up everyone in the palace. Her mother Elizabeth rushed straight to her daughter's bedroom. Fear had found a place to nestle inside her heart. She hurried inside the room and gasped in horror. There was blood scattered everywhere, a head rolling on the floor, intestines hanging out, Tiffany's lung was cut in half, and her non-beating heart was not in her mother's sight. *Woosh!* Something scurried passed her, growling from every direction. Bloodied footprints created a path.

"Aah!" shrieked Elizabeth, never to be seen...

Khadeejah Ruwaydah Shaffi (12)

Manor High School, Oadby

THE SPY

I sank into the brown cashmere chair, smiling. I had worked two months for what I'd call the highest-end undercover company. The FBI had nothing on us; we had around 2,000 members, all based underground. In those couple of months, not only had I accomplished three 'degree A' missions, but managed to single-handedly murder a whole team plotting against us. Mass murder may be fun, but I don't regret retiring.

"So what brings you here?" The shrill voice made me jump.

Clearing my throat, I began, "I was hoping to apply as the nursery teacher... if the role's still available."

Umaymah Esat (13)

Manor High School, Oadby

A LIFE OF MYSTERY!

"Guilty!" the judge announced as he thumped the gavel against the wooden board. The daunting man screamed as he was dragged reluctantly across the frigid floors. An hour passed and his ragged shirt reeked of iron and gruel but nevertheless, he pondered amongst himself as he laid his head down and eyed the discoloured walls. Beaten, guards complained as they walked past but what could be done? He glanced towards the metal bars and they glanced back menacingly, cackling peculiarly. He stood up, and with blistered fingers pacing the wall, he murmured to himself. He stopped. This is the way!

Harsh Parmar (12)
Manor High School, Oadby

HIDDEN HERO

Buildings fall to the ground as families sob at the sight of their homes crashing and crumbling. All is chaos and destruction. Through the rubble and dust, a figure emerges, instantly bringing a smile to everyone's face - a superhero. I've never understood. All this time I've been seen as the evil monster, whilst superheroes wreck so much and get away with anything with the excuse of saving the world. Always just reinforcing the damage already caused by humans. Without me, they could never be stopped! Still, I am the enemy, the hated one. The misunderstood, hidden hero.

Summer Jones (12)
Manor High School, Oadby

LONELY

I'm lonely. Always have been, always will be. Sittin' in my maze, waiting for someone to come. When someone does, I get attacked. I have to defend myself, it's not my fault I'm so strong. And then I'm the villain? I don't get it. How come all my mates are free, somewhere else, and I'm stuck in 'ere? And I've 'eard some lad's comin' to chop my 'ead off or something. This time, I want a fight though, why not? It's been a long time since I've actually wanted to kill someone. Who am I? I am the Minotaur...

Tommy Blacklaws (13)
Manor High School, Oadby

THE WRATH OF THE WIND

It wasn't the wind's fault. The azure winds embraced the heartfelt village, hugging it, squeezing it tight. On the fluorescent hill, the village flourished, its windmills dancing with the wind's joy. The villagers cherished the winds, yet still demanded it for their every need. Every single word toppled amongst the wind. The wind grew colder and harsher, the youthful joy it once held slowly becoming a bitter husk of what it once was. It was enough. The winds embraced the town, but without the joy it once held. It was not a warm embrace, yet it was a strangling storm.

Emily Appleton-Corbett (12)
Manor High School, Oadby

HOW I NEVER FITTED IN...

I've never really fitted in. Even in the orphanage. I had my revenge even then. Nobody really knew how John Cruppet was hung from the balcony. Or how Suzy Binns was strangled to death with her yo-yo. That left everyone in the orphanage completely befuddled. But that's in the past. Since then, I've killed 369 victims and nobody has ever seen me. That news reporter who criticised my murders? Pfft. She didn't even see who killed her. Anyway, watch out for these murders. I could well be killing someone now. I could be perched outside your window right now, waiting...

Mohammed Hussain Dhiraj (13)

Manor High School, Oadby

THE UNKNOWN ERROR

Anticipation, agitation, antsy; the uncertainty filled her for they were out there. Watching her every movement, hearing her every word. Disguised to fulfil her liking, yet now it was clear they were nothing but a facade. Feeling as if she failed herself by falling victim to masked manipulative deeds. Each one of her interests, her hobbies, they knew. Superfluous thoughts occupied her mind, though it all could have been prevented: if only she had remembered to click mere buttons. 'Virus Alert!' the screen silently screamed as they gained control. There was no going back.

Aaisha Mamsa (15)

Manor High School, Oadby

FEAR

It's eating away my humanity. I'm trying to grasp onto it, but I can't prevent it from slipping away from me. This virus isn't what I intended... I search for help, but I'm infecting everyone in sight. The lights flicker. It's coming. Frantically, my eyes glance over my dad's research documents. I thought it would be in here. Occasionally, I give up hope, I think the cure is non-existent. Whispers beckon to me to come closer, I can't resist turning the doorknob. I know I shouldn't, doom is waiting. The tension tears me apart. I turn around...

Tamira Keshav (12)
Manor High School, Oadby

THE WOLF MEETS THE WITCHES OF RED RIDING WOOD

They stood around me in a menacing ring. Twenty-four witches altogether; young, old, tall, small witches. Of course, these witches were centuries old and had concerned themselves with the goings-on of Red Riding Hood's woods for just as long. So here I was, in a witch's room, with a boiling kettle as company. I had, supposedly, done a terrible thing by killing Red Riding Hood, her grandma and the woodcutter who came to help. The witches had decided. They would write a book showing my death as the big bad wolf. Their version of events. That's the story you know.

Isla Reiff-Marganiec (13)
Manor High School, Oadby

LUCIFER'S CALL

I remember sitting down on the bench next to the corpse, cold and still, its organs pulled out, drying out on the eve of summer. The perfect time. My hands, covered in scarlet blood, felt alive, satisfied from pulling the flesh out of the victim, to cover myself and keep away from the cold whispers of the lady. The one standing right next to me, her face wasted. Her eyes, burnt right through her deformed cranium. She wore a stygian cloth, covering everything except for her ominous face, she wailed in a blood-curdling way.

"The devil made me do it..."

Navjot Singh (14)

Manor High School, Oadby

THE AFTERMATH OF THE CLOWN PRINCE OF CRIME

Sat there, looking at himself in his mirror, tears streaming down his face, he thought, *why does everyone despise me? Everyone knows me as The Joker, with bright purple clothes and devilish-looking make-up. I just want to be forgiven.* He went outside to get some air. Everyone he went past trembled in fear. He came across a gang of armed men. He just shoved past to be immediately thrown onto the ground. The men pulled their guns out. Joker felt shocks piercing his body. He closed his eyes, finally resting. The one thing he could never do. Silence...

Aryan Kalsi (12)
Manor High School, Oadby

THE TRUE VILLAIN

I never really belonged on Asgard. Especially after my own father turned me into a villain. I was face to face with my 'father' Odin. In his hand, a clear, ragged crystal. Suddenly, a blinding white light shot out like lightning. A ribbon of magic reached towards me and slithered into my ear, a sharp, piercing sound overwhelming my mind. My head felt numb. Paralysed. I could still hear the shouts of Thor that day, still taste the guilt on my tongue and feel the pain. But Thor would never understand. Nor would he believe that his father controlled me.

Ella Laidlow (13)
Manor High School, Oadby

BROKEN: ROCK, PAPER, SCISSORS

In less than a minute, hundreds of trees were slaughtered. I was fearless, as I was the one in power. I am Scissors, the pitiless barbarian, hoping for destruction and tremendous devastation. Mercilessly, I sprinted across the dense trees, searching for my target. Staring ahead, I could see her: Paper. Panic rose in her chest. Fear choked in her face. I vowed to complete what I came for. It was my moment: the moment where I would destroy my inauspicious prey. Suddenly, a bulky creature jumped right above me, until I was crushed to death. It was Rock...

Alia Megahed (11)

Manor High School, Oadby

FOREST

Tree trunks swirled around the man. My eyes streaked with blood. The forest was now in my control, my hands swayed back and forth moving the trees with them. Blood dripped from the man's hands as if he had been sliced. His body was covered in black, venomous blood. It came away from the head. Suddenly a man came from behind, putting an oily hand which was cut into so many pieces the grains of sand in the world couldn't compare.

I turned around and saw the mask. I knew what was happening. He'd come for what was rightfully his.

Muhammad-Hudhayfah Shaffi (13)
Manor High School, Oadby

ATOP THE ESTATE...

I waited in the rain for hours atop the estate, planning what I would do to them once they arrived. Just imagining their gouged-out eyes in my hands made me... chuckle. Even though my knuckles would bleed and ache, even though my legs would be cut and bruised, even though tears would be seeping out of my tired eyes, I would still smile after seeing their pathetic, dead corpses. Crimson blood would be streaming out of their wounds, dripping down onto the nearby civilians, clueless that their dazzling hero had been defeated and destroyed.

Florence Davies (12)
Manor High School, Oadby

HOW I ENDED UP DESTROYING THE UNIVERSE

Down it goes into the bottomless pit, never to be seen again they thought. The pit wasn't bottomless but held a deadly monster so powerful that he could destroy the whole universe one million times just with one breath. He was the second most powerful ancient relic. So far he had been dormant for aeons. Guess what. They just dropped the only thing that could wake it up and also quadruple his power. Not a single person is alive to stop him, not even the most powerful ancient relic and the original power source of everything can.

Issa (12)
Manor High School, Oadby

WAITING

When he first hit me, I screamed. Second time, I cried. Third time, I stopped. I didn't do anything. Couldn't do anything. All I had left was to wait. Wait as he hit me over and over and over. Wait as I bled and bruised and broke. Wait until I couldn't. Wait until I snapped. Wait until the knife slipped through him. Wait until I found myself standing over him, steel in hand, glistening red. I made him bleed, made him bruise, made him break. Because of him, he was the first. And because of him, he wasn't the last.

Zaynah Chohan (14)
Manor High School, Oadby

NO FACE

He walked up to me slowly as I trembled in fear. The devious man had no facial features, like eyes or lips. Just a head with two dents where eyes would be. He cunningly laughed as he got closer, clutching his hands together and a dark essence appeared on his fingertips. He was wearing a long black coat covering his whole body. The footsteps echoed as the man reached me. I turned to run. Suddenly I felt something cold against my back. I looked down at my stomach, I realised the dark essence had cut through me. I collapsed. Dead.

Dipinder Singh (12)
Manor High School, Oadby

DEATH'S DISEASE, HUMANITY'S CURE

People often view me as evil, but I'm just doing my job. They make stories of me, of how Death is evil, how to evade me. But now, humanity has created a disease that destroys me, but cures them, deeming them immortal. I simply can not allow this. I can't just abjure, the boss won't allow it. I'll have to find a way, but how do I kill something which isn't even alive? Now I know. I kill the person who made it. Who was it again... Adolf Hitler? No... Oh yes. It's Saad. I'm coming for you.

Saad Moolakadai
Manor High School, Oadby

HAWKINS LAB - THE ORIGINS OF DR BRENNER

I knew I was a special child. I could do things with my mind. My parents undermined me, saying I'm like all other captive children at the lab. As my unbothered parents continued to test children like me, the gate opened at the hands of one. Suddenly, the back of my neck tingled, it felt like I was being hit by a bitter gust of wind. It might have been hours or mere seconds. Halt. He likes it cold. Time to show my parents my worth; a trip to the Upside Down. They better remember my name... Dr Martin Brenner.

Tania Nathan (13)
Manor High School, Oadby

VICIOUS VOLCANO VILLAIN

Lying in slumber. Lying to all who have come and gone, from the Roman, Greeks and Celts. My name is Eyjafjallajokull. I have been deceiving those who have come and have died, but today two million years, eight months, twenty-four days, six hours and counting and I am ready to explode and let the world be reborn anew. I am ready to blow and destroy all of humanity after years of deceit. Science will not stop me nor even my mother, the Earth or my brothers, the land and the sea. No one can stop me, I am invincible!

Umar Salah (12)
Manor High School, Oadby

REVENGE WILL BE MINE

Blood, blood, blood. Pools of redness around me. The rotten stench of bodies near me as I cry and cry. The face that killed my parents and my siblings. Leaving me stranded without anyone to help me. Letting me curse myself to get revenge to give her the same misery that she gave me. Leaving her all alone in this world. How come she finds love?! How come she gets her happily ever after?! I will get my revenge! I will get my happily ever after. As the saying goes an eye for an eye, a family for a family...

Mohammed Adam Galeriya (14)
Manor High School, Oadby

DEATH'S PRISON

I sit alone, isolated, devastated, with only the forgotten souls to keep me company. Their troubled whispers trap me. I can only feel sorry for them. If only they knew death is a mere slave who is compelled to obey the formidable evil. If only I could free myself of this curse. All of mankind sees me as a villain, a malevolent figure. I have accepted the fact that this barren land of despair will forever be my home. I look around at my eerie prison. The metal bars encasing all sadness, all devastation.

Zara Patel (13)

Manor High School, Oadby

THE CORN MAZE

I ran from the house I'd been encaged within for the past three months. He had me locked in the building for so long. This was my chance to break free. I swung the front door open and ran. I was sprinting through the corn mazes as fast as I could. I could feel the sweat running down my back. I had no idea which direction I was going in. I stopped about half a mile into the cornfield for a break. I was exhausted. *Silence.* I was convinced it was safe. All of a sudden... someone grabbed me.

Sriya Panesar (15)
Manor High School, Oadby

THE HAUNTING SEA

I was on my way to England when I woke up to a whistling sound. I went to the dock to see if someone was there. From the corner of my eye, I saw a boy with bright blue eyes and black sparkling scales all around his body. He had sharp teeth and an evil grin on his face. He told me, "You shouldn't have come to this part of the sea." He sounded like a horrifying monster. Just then, he jumped on board and turned into a human with normal teeth and dark brown hair covered in seaweed.

Safiyyah Nasim (12)
Manor High School, Oadby

ONE BETRAYAL TWO MYSTERIES

I was playing at Rapunzel's tower with my friends, Rapunzel, Ariel, Snow White, Cinderella, Aurora and Jasmine. Rapunzel said something really weird to me.

She said, "I'm going for a walk and don't let anybody follow me." I was definitely going to follow her and not long after, I saw her talking to Maleficent. She nodded very motionlessly and nodded very vacantly. She was coming back. I ran back to Rapunzel's tower and told the other girls what had happened.

Kavi Parmar (12)

Manor High School, Oadby

SWAP

1879 was the year of his death, everyone was devastated for months. I wasn't... Here's what happened. Back in 1879, I went on a walk and saw this old, dirty, smelly guy. He asked if I wanted to 'swap'. I was so confused he kept repeating this. Later that day, I went to bed and heard it again. "Swap." And again, "Swap." I had to say yes or he would still be saying it... I suddenly woke up trying to catch my breath. I got drenched.

Storme Jarvis (13)
Manor High School, Oadby

A SIREN'S TALE

Circe spread the rumour that we attracted sailors with our songs so they would crash on our shores and then we would devour them. She even convinced Odysseus. But we can't leave this place, so our people gather on the coasts and sing whenever ships come too close. We try to warn them that we are an island of flowers - there is no food. But it does not matter how many times we sing, they still come. They crash on our shores and perish.

David Howard (11)
Medina College, Newport

MALEFICENT

Alone. I'm alone again. The hopes and dreams have been torn away. The anger and hate are so strong but yet my heart is so madly in love. I don't want to be evil, I don't want to be the character everyone is afraid of. I want peace. I want peace more than anyone. It's been decades since my last horror. A lot of things have changed. I'm a leader today. I help people. However, there's times when I feel anger and I try to fight it every day. But I'm tired. I just need the end.

Isobel Harrison (14)
My Learning Journey, Askern

THE DEVIL'S DAY OFF

Based on the game 'Cuphead'

I'm taking a break today. Not a big deal, I could get that cup's soul any day. Even King Dice, my right-hand man is taking a break, so they won't be airing 'Roll the Dice' tonight. Even Stickler the, may I point out very annoying auditor, is taking a break. In fact, I even shut the Carnevil (play on words of carnival and evil) for the day so I won't be collecting any souls today at all.

"You winning again boss?" I hear King Dice's voice ask.

"No," I reply.

He leaves so then I enjoy my day off.

Brandon Atkinson (11)

Norham High School, North Shields

THE UNKNOWN KIDNAPPING

For the past 18 years my only view has been four mouldy green walls. Each day I was lucky if I was given a sandwich to eat. Some days he forgot entirely and I felt sick with hunger. The painful cramping in my stomach, a reminder that I hadn't eaten in three days. My only company was the dripping of the leaking sink in my shed. I had been only 11 when I was taken and by the scrawled line in my diary, I am 29 now. An adult, no longer a child. I wasn't rescued, I ran away. Freedom.

Samantha Hope (11)
Norham High School, North Shields

EMOTION

There was blood. On his hands. It poured and pooled in rivulets, vermillion and scarlet. But he felt nothing, nothing staring at the three, lifeless bodies stretched out in front of him, nothing staring at his hands, congealing blood clinging in desperation to his fingertips. He felt nothing in the silence, screams still echoing off the walls. Beautiful anguish. He felt empty. But, for a second, for those wonderful moments snatched in between the fragile bridge of life and death, he felt whole, a warmth spilling against his ribs like a dam overflow. And for a second, he smiled.

Katherine Ingleton (15)
North Bridge House Senior School And Sixth Form, Islington

TWISTS AND TURNS

Outrageous, agonising, excruciating pain made its way through my vicious soul. Who was I? What had I turned into? I remained oblivious of the tragedy sealed within my brutal fate. My raging anguish controlled me, clutching onto my identity as if I were clutching onto my last hope. My heart slowly departed my body unconsciously. I had become part of the gruesome curse that foreshadowed us. Portrayed as a monstrosity determined to welcome despair. My life dismantled itself, as I unwillingly became the cause of everyone's misery. Though they believe it is them, it is us that remain the victims.

Ridhi Choudhary (14)
Olchfa School, Sketty

TECHNOLOGY

Technology always was a double-edged sword, and the ILOVEYOU virus was no exception. That was the popular name for it. The geeks that created it called it the Melissa Virus, and it swept the world. A byte-sized virus was all it took. Everyone fell for it. Everyone was curious. Everyone opened that one email.

'Hope You Like My vIrUs.

LOVE-LETTER-FOR-YOU.

Better You Than Me Buddy.'

It only took a few days to stop it, but the damage was already done. Over fifty million computers were infected. Over ten billion dollars in damages.

Luca Necsoiu (13)

Onslow St Audrey's School, Hatfield

BA'AL'S SAGA

Evil... A profound and hypocritical concept created to satisfy humanity's thirst for violence, bloodshed and death. The longer you study 'good', 'evil' and 'peace', the more you realise that the only things that truly exist in this accursed reality are merely pain, suffering and futility. That is what I've learned from my predecessors. My sole motivation is to vanquish this being that proclaims itself as God, because to kill this 'God' would free this futile reality of unnecessary and worthless concepts which would only leave behind eternal truth and prove that I, Ba'al, am the only true and noble being.

Eyad Ali (14)

Ormiston Victory Academy, Norwich

THE KILLER'S STORY

There I was, caught. My brother, the golden child, mother in the stands. "Don't say it," she mouthed. I nodded.

The judge turned to me and said, "Mr Smith, anything to say for yourself?"

Silence.

My mind rushing, choking back tears, sweating.

"Mr Smith?"

I couldn't take any more of this. I stood up, tears rushing down my cheeks and yelled, "It was them, they made me, they hurt me for 18 years and forced me to kill! They made me who I am!"

Silence fell through the courtroom once more. The judge in shock, my brother yelled, "You liar!"

Katlyn Reynolds-Fish (13)
Ormiston Victory Academy, Norwich

TWO-FACED

It's finally my day off, what a delightful day! I step into the station and enter my office. I'm instantly surrounded and praised. "You're in the newspaper! We're so close to figuring this villain out."

Ha! If only they knew... Everything I ask, they answer eagerly. Everything I request, they rush to present to me. It's an amusing hobby, but I could not do it full-time. Too much admiration.

Finally, at the end of the day when I've finally finished deceiving my chasers, I head back to continue my 'immoral plan against the world' as the newspaper would put it...

Fatimah Alsaiari (15)
Ormiston Victory Academy, Norwich

FINALLY VICTORIOUS

Finally, I was standing directly across from my childhood friend, my one true enemy... the hero. My eyes were locked on hers, she had tears brimming in her eyes, hair messy, clothes wrecked. I ruined her reputation for final validation. I should be the one praised, not her, never her. Ever since we were young she had *everything*, leaving me with... nothing. The rumours online, blackmail, dedication to ruin her finally came together. I was going to take her spotlight, her praise. Everything would finally be mine. She's now suffering from abandonment and that made me ecstatic. She's finally gone.

Elizabeth Foy (12)
Ormiston Victory Academy, Norwich

MOTIVATION

I can't stop being Death. I don't even remember what I did to get here, it's been too long. As I walk through the dark streets, overflowing with souls, I can't help but wish I was anywhere but where I was about to be.

"Hello?" The little girl's spirit stands in front of me.

"Hello." I hold my hand out and she takes it hesitantly.

"Where are we going? Where's my parents?" she asks me, her voice shaking as she does so.

"I'm sorry," I say as I lead her away from where she died. I can't stop being Death.

Leah Bruce (14)
Ormiston Victory Academy, Norwich

THE LIFE OF GINNY CAMERON

It all started with a well-known, harmful facility. They took small and young children and made them into war machines. Unfortunately, Ginny Cameron was one of them. They gave her unbelievable powers that could change the world. But the facility had other plans. She was sent on missions that were basically killing sprees.

This went on non-stop until a lovely lady came to help Ginny. The lady brought Ginny to her home after she got Ginny under control. Surprisingly, the lady had awesome technology and it made Ginny stronger and gave her control over her powers. Ginny was finally happy.

Agata Elmanowska (11)

Ormiston Victory Academy, Norwich

WHAT IS A MOTIVE?

The flashing red and blue, I remember it vividly. They'd finally caught me. My 'reign of terror' was over. The lights in that interrogation room were too bright, almost blinding. I could barely even focus. And that's when they asked, "Why?"

That was a good question. Why did I do it? I wonder about that every day. Should I feel shame? Remorse? Guilt? When I remained silent they asked again. They were so desperate for a motive, it was almost amusing, but I had no motive to give them. Do you know why? Well, I'm not in charge, he is.

Scarlett Featherby (14)
Ormiston Victory Academy, Norwich

THE TRUTH BEHIND CINDERELLA

I still haven't forgotten Cinderella. I miss her, I do, and everything she did for me. I realise now how badly I treated her. She never deserved anything I put her through and I wish I would've been more of a mother figure for her. Cinderella was going through such a hard time and my jealousy of her took over both of our lives. Cinderella was the prettiest, most precious, warm-hearted girl. My daughters took jealousy to another level and I went along to make my daughters feel better, but I shouldn't have. I want her to know I'm sorry.

Harmony Pitt (14)
Ormiston Victory Academy, Norwich

THE SURGERY

I never really belonged in the life I was given. Pressured to be the perfect daughter until I wasn't. I'd had enough. My mother would beat me if I didn't look or act utterly perfect. As I grew older, the more my looks grew unbearable. Something had to change or my mother would hate me forever. I got plastic surgery, it was my only choice. My surgeon wasn't qualified and destroyed my face. I looked like a decaying zombie.
I had to hide myself from the world. All of the laughing and staring turned me mad, very mad, and evil.

Lilly Mortimer (12)
Ormiston Victory Academy, Norwich

RIGHT VS WRONG

I did it to survive. I did it because I thought it was right. It was a way of continuing my family's legacy. I've always been taught that killing people who kill others is right. If this is my belief, then how am I the bad guy? The 'heroes' who stop me don't know right from wrong. Kill after kill, they never succeed. They always fail, never win against the 'bad guys'. The villains are the real masterminds behind the plans, never to fail. We always escape the clutches of the heroes. We are the real heroes in this story...

Ted Shorter (13)
Ormiston Victory Academy, Norwich

MOTHER GOTHEL'S STORY

I never really belonged. I never felt beautiful or pretty and I never felt included. But, taking her completed me. It felt as if the hole in my heart was full; she kept me young and irresistible. Finally, for the first time in my life, I belonged. Rapunzel saved me.

Every day we'd sing her magical song. "Flower gleam and glow, let your power shine..."

One day, I was ageing quite quickly. I panicked and sang her magical song. It failed. We sang it again. It went wrong. Why had it broken? I used it ten times this hour! Sorry!

Abigail Watts (14)

Ormiston Victory Academy, Norwich

THE WINTER'S FROST

It was one frosty winter's evening when a child was stolen from its home. A pale white sheet of snow lay peacefully on the land. No footprints to be seen...

It'd been about three weeks since the little boy was seen with an old lady. They were crossing the street, heading to the graveyard...

We fast-forwarded two weeks. The little boy was found under the glimmering snow, torn and stiff, with his blood staining the snow pink. When questioned by the cops she said that she killed him because he was good and she was the opposite...

Megan-Sue Robinson (13)
Ormiston Victory Academy, Norwich

THE WITCH CAPTURES

A girl named Emily liked to play near a funny-looking cottage. She made a bad mistake and knocked on the door and something dragged her in. She screamed then she saw an old lady. In front of her was a cauldron. She was shocked. Then she screamed again until the old lady laughed. It sounded familiar. She screamed, "Witch!"
Then the witch smiled and said, "You are under my roof, you're under my rules."
Emily ran. The witch ran after her and put her in a cage and then the cauldron. Emily was never seen again.

Melissa Davies (12)
Ormiston Victory Academy, Norwich

AFTER EVER AFTER

I still haven't forgotten the day Batman died. It was a tragic day for the city of Gotham and me. You may be wondering why me? Well, we were enemies, now I have a new one, a pathetic little teenager who goes by the name of Robin! Now he's right in front of me. "Why didn't you save him?" I scream.

"Why does it matter? Plus he was going to die anyway."

"How could you say that?" I say. And with that, I pull out my knife and charge towards him and he approaches me. A new rivalry is born...

Jude Putt (13)

Ormiston Victory Academy, Norwich

WHO'S THE REAL VILLAIN?

That superhero act was a lie. She only pretended to be good to find out their plans to help save the world and avoid getting caught. She turned her back on the heroes and turned to the villains. She left and joined their plan to destroy Earth, until she was stopped by one of the heroes from before. Bubbles pounced at Ivory, breaking her vines, she swiped back. She crawled to the button, hoping to blow up the Earth. Bubbles pounced again, this time leaving her lying lifeless and not breathing. He walked over her body as a heroic hero.

Jessica Ryan (13)
Ormiston Victory Academy, Norwich

MINION MADNESS

I never really belonged in this group because every other Minion was a different size. So I felt left out and I didn't fit in. Every day I'm sad because I want to be a whole other person, even though I should be happy with who I am. But I'm not. I want to be a different person. Other Minions make fun of me, like Carl would say 'you obviously weren't made for this group' and 'have you seen what it's like at this height? It's so much better than where you are'. All the Minions bully me every day.

Phoenix Sergent (13)
Ormiston Victory Academy, Norwich

MY DAY OFF

Today I am having a day off annoying people and stealing them. The first thing I am going to do is to watch my favourite TV programme where some young people are annoying others and stealing them. Next, I am going to try baking my favourite chocolate cupcakes and eat them in front of homeless kids to make them feel hungry and sad. Then I'll sleep for about four hours so I'm ready for my adventure to steal ice cream from the ice cream truck. Finally, I will end my day by drinking some hot tears from a child's eyes.

Rokaia Elgishy (13)
Ormiston Victory Academy, Norwich

PLANKTON'S FAILURE

Finally, I was about to win. I was so close to receiving the secret recipe. I could hear somebody walking in. I was terrified. I tried to hide on one of the beams of the restaurant. I walked on the ceiling with my equipment but then he saw me.

I fell down in horror and SpongeBob grabbed me and beat me up. He kicked me back into the Chum Bucket. I was defeated. *Why is this so difficult?* I thought.

I went back for round two but Squidward was by the door while SpongeBob was inspecting the damage I'd caused.

Tyler Woodhouse

Ormiston Victory Academy, Norwich

NEVERLAND OR NEVER LEAVE?

Villain? Why am I the villain in everyone's eyes? See, villain and hero are two sides of the same coin. They saw me as the villain whilst underneath I was trying to help. I had an old friend called Peter. We discovered a beautiful land where we could stay young and bask in the light of magical pixie dust. But he got greedy. Forcing people to join us. Damning them to eternity. For what? So he could be seen as superior.

I take a step to save someone and get pushed back three. No one sees why it's called Neverland.

Kiki Fairhead (13)

Ormiston Victory Academy, Norwich

THIS IS WAR

I still haven't forgotten the day my brothers and family fell. A bloodbath of warriors, our kingdom fell. One man escaped alive, and that was myself.

After escaping to a faraway land, I had to cope with the loss of everything. Sitting in the cave in the mountain, I looked out at the setting sun. Deep down I knew that the rogue kingdom had been looking for me all these years. The sun disappeared beneath the horizon and I was bathed in the faint light of the moon. I turned my back to head inside. Then the war cry...

Ethan Hunn (14)

Ormiston Victory Academy, Norwich

NOT SO BIG AND BAD...

If I never turned into a monster, what would my life be like? Can I still be with my daughter and my loving wife? They call me the 'Big Bad Wolf', the freak who roams the woods. I didn't want to be this. I wanted a normal life, living with my family and caring for my sick mother. I didn't even mean to eat him. It was just... instinct.

But my hunger grows. There's this cottage nearby. I need to be quick. A little girl in a bright red cloak is approaching. But she looks too much like my daughter...

Jahred Socao (13)
Ormiston Victory Academy, Norwich

BEHIND THE SCENES

My heart was pounding before I went on stage.
"Action!"
I got into character and started to go along with it. It was
going well until my eyes blurred and everything started
moving. I fell and hit the ground like a bunch of stones. I
woke up in hospital, but something was off. I went and
looked in the mirror and my eyes were red and my head was
green. I couldn't speak but then my stomach rumbled and I
was craving people! That's when I lost my mind and was
looking around looking for someone...

Daisy-Mai Turner-Lodge (12)

Ormiston Victory Academy, Norwich

VICTORIOUS VILLAINS

Finally, I was about to win when a muscle man came and fought off the grizzly bear. When they finished, the man was seriously hurt and the bear was injured. I went over to the man to see how injured he was... I looked at the man and it was my father.

Twenty years earlier, my dad gave me powers of prophecy to see into the future and I wish he hadn't...

I picked him up and said, "Where were you?" Suddenly I saw a vision of the bear and it had blood on its mouth and flesh... Father's flesh...

Liberty Nicholls (13)
Ormiston Victory Academy, Norwich

CTHULU'S SPARE TIME

After a long night of ruthless waves and storms, I needed to take my mind off of it all and unwind. Now I, Cthulu, probably don't seem like the type of guy to have a hobby or pastime, but I must admit I adore making miniature boats in glass bottles. Kinda embarrassing, I know, but where do you think all the tiny bottles that you throw into the sea with letters in go? That's why I destroy boats as well. A tad violent, I suppose, but what else can I do? It's rather lonely down here on the seabed sometimes.

Jasmine Hill (14)
Ormiston Victory Academy, Norwich

FAIR IS FAIR

What makes a hero? How do you define people? You have to look a certain way to be expelled. Your actions don't matter, only your looks.

Me and Suzan used to be best friends but that was destroyed in under a minute. We both should be to blame for the crimes we committed but all it took was puppy dog eyes and I was blamed. Set up by the person I believed I was going to spend my whole life with. Betrayed.

But mark my words, I will be remembered forever. Because fair is fair as long as you're pretty.

Daisy Cooper (14)
Ormiston Victory Academy, Norwich

HARLEQUIN

You may know me as Harley Quinn, but you don't know my backstory. I did it to survive. I have people after me. Many people. I didn't know what to do except kill anyone coming for me. The crazy people from the asylum, they're crazy and scary. They have a psychotic laugh. The asylum is dark and damp. I now live in silence, no one after me. I'm happy I have the Joker. I'm scared, I don't want to go back to killing, it's mentally draining and I'm far more happy. I can't go back.

Bethany Hawkins (12)
Ormiston Victory Academy, Norwich

THE MISFIT

I was never the same as everyone else. For many years I was nice then changed. I started by stealing money to then stealing stuff like material for clothes. Tomorrow I'll be working what I thought would be the best dream job. However, instead of working in a fashion store, I'm cleaning it which means I'll have to work my way up.
I realise I can steal everything and create my own fashion. I like that idea so I do. I steal most material and make everything. I have to find a way to get noticed.

Tegan Blanchflower (13)
Ormiston Victory Academy, Norwich

THE GOSS' REVENGE

Just months before I was born my father accepted a fight against a German boxing legend by the name of Otto Kapitan. Round one was going smoothly for my father until round two, Otto threw many illegal hits, causing my father to fall and never get up.

Today is my fight and I must prove to the world that the Gosses are on top and I will make sure he doesn't get up just like my father. My fight is against Otto's son, my enemy. I will make sure Otto feels the same pain I feel. I will end him.

Joshua Goss (14)
Ormiston Victory Academy, Norwich

THE CRUEL REALITY

The year 2328. The world had changed... People started to get powers. I was unlucky, I had no powers, it was quite rare, but I was bullied by the powerful. It was a world based on hierarchy. Along with the powers came heroes. Heroes only cared for the strong, but took the title 'heroes' for the money and fame, but every story has a villain. That is me. I kill these so-called heroes, not for the title of villain but to help the weak. I was bullied and put in my place but that did not stop me...

Elisha Brookes (13)

Ormiston Victory Academy, Norwich

CRUELLA

I haven't always been like this you know. I used to be a
normal person. At some point I changed. I started to steal
dogs, well, only Dalmatians. I only stole for the money but
then it was for property. I even had thoughts about using
them for their fur to make stuff. This mainy started because
I was bullied at school for being poor and how I dressed. It
was so unfair, I always thought I had to change so I did, just
not in a good way, but for the worst. I just couldn't change,
it was horrible.

Ella Futter (13)
Ormiston Victory Academy, Norwich

JOKER'S BACKSTORY

I never really belonged in Gotham City, back in school I was bullied a lot for what I looked like.

One day in high school it was sports day and I was chosen for an event. Let me tell you now, it didn't go well... I was made fun of for the rest of my life.

That's when I got revenge. I got some face paint, I may have looked like a bad clown, that's when I got my nickname 'Joker', as you know me now. I killed all of my enemies. People assume I'm bad but I'm not.

Jadon Lord (12)
Ormiston Victory Academy, Norwich

RECOVERY

I have taken this too far. I have messed up, I know I have. I'm not like this on the inside, I've only been doing this to impress people, I have completely ruined my town, my hometown. The billboard fully wrecked and destroyed trees have lost colour. Oh why have I done this? I'm going to fix this mess!

I grab a hat to cover my face. I fly out the window, shooting and lifting trees, billboards, everything. The whole town watches me fix our homes, the town's now beautiful.

Sophia Cracknell (13)

Ormiston Victory Academy, Norwich

THE VILLAIN

Jerry and Tim were practising their superpowers and then they heard a glass break, it was Bob! He came and used his superpowers to pick stuff up and throw it at Tim and Jerry. Jerry got mad and picked up a glass bottle and broke it, so it was sharp as he was about to throw it. Bob picked him up and launched him out the window of the building. Tim was terrified and hid in the corner. Bob realised what he had done and said sorry then he flew away, he was never seen ever again.

Koen Spinks (12)
Ormiston Victory Academy, Norwich

SCAR THE KING

Finally, I was about to win in a fight with my brother Mufasa to be the king. I'd always wanted to be king because everyone loved him. I was jealous and mad, I wanted to be him and wished I was perfect. Nobody cheered for me being the king of the zoo. But in the end I controlled everyone.

Hannah Rallos (12)
Ormiston Victory Academy, Norwich

I AM A VILLAIN

I am a villain. I know, but hear me out. I have my reasons.
My evil mum tried to make the world think I was ugly.
Horrible I know. But you'll never believe what happened
next. They believed her! How dare they!? And so you'll never
guess what I did. I went insane trying to prove them wrong.
But guess what, I failed, I failed! I killed the Dalmatians and
made them into a fur coat. A beautiful one might I add. And
now they think I am not only ugly but evil too.

Isabelle Hough (12)
Outwood Academy Newbold, Chesterfield

LYSANDRE'S ROCKET

It was late at night, four days after the initial earthquake warning. There were only three days until it was scheduled to hit. I'd had little time to construct the weapon but I couldn't waste the opportunity. Burying the rocket, I stared around at the destruction my first weapon caused. That was when Team Flare was at its greatest, and I felt unstoppable. That was a long time ago. Anyway, here was the plan: the earthquake strikes, my rocket absorbs energy from the quake and launches upwards, then it releases all the energy in shockwaves and destroys all of Kalos!

Joe Gifford (13)
Poole Grammar School, Poole

THE ABSOLUTE GOOD GUY

It is I, Mr Wolf, the star of two well-known tales about me, the absolute good guy. Oh, you don't think I'm good? I can explain! Well, my jaws went for their natural instincts at that poor Miss Riding Hood's house, and my serious asthma got out of control when visiting those pigs. Oh, you still don't believe I'm the good guy, do you? Let's try this. When not visiting my friendly pigs, I enjoy sipping blood, sorry, plum juice. I devour tasty pigs, sorry, figs. And I play with people's skin, sorry, kin. Am I really that bad?

Lucas Turnbull (12)
Poole Grammar School, Poole

RELEASE OF THE DINOSAURS

Finally. I was in. I had a job in Jurassic Park security, and everyone was out of the room. I savoured the moment, slurping my cola as I clicked the button to lock the others out and turned off the security. Instantly klaxons blared and red lights flashed. I didn't care. Because it felt appropriate I screamed: "I am Dennis Nedry! I broke Jurassic Park!" I flicked the camera switch and watched as chaos overruled all. There was banging at the doors but I didn't care. I had won. I would get the dinosaur creation serum.

Jack Oseland (13)
Poole Grammar School, Poole

JOKER RETURNS

I knew that I had to make right what I had done wrong to Gotham City over all these years. Me, the Joker, I'm going to run a clown competition and whoever comes in the best outfit will win. To enter the competition, you shall pay 5. What I'll do to make up for everything I've done, all the buildings I've destroyed, all the destruction I've caused, I'll give all the money raised from this competition to the poor of Gotham City.

Now my time has come... Not even Batman can stop me.

Finn Charles (11)
Poole Grammar School, Poole

HADES, GOD OF HELL

Hercules launched himself against the entrance to Hades' castle, but the doors weren't budging. After many tries it opened. Then he searched for Cerberus' room. Hades woke up to a loud bang coming from the room below. He raced downstairs only to discover that Hercules had broken into the castle! "Hercules!" Hades yelled. "What are you doing in my home?"
Hercules froze. He was caught. Hades launched two slimy, writing snakes at him, then sent him back to the mortal realm. He rushed to Cerberus' room. Hades sighed with relief. His guard dog and best friend was safe.

Saffron Bright (14)
Redborne Upper School & Community College, Ampthill

THE BLIND CHILD

He stands there, pale as frost, fragile as china. Another ignorant soul trapped in my graveyard of stone. The snakes surrounding my deadly eyes revel in the addition to our collection. I turn my back to his fearful face, to see another peering at me from between the snarling rocks. Small hands, small clothes, too small for a knight. And yet they can stare, even when I stare back. White eyes. Closed eyes. Blind eyes.

They crawl out from their hidden hole. Bruises brandish their skin. They reach out a hand, and I defy my principles, taking it in mine.

Ffion Harris (14)
Redborne Upper School & Community College, Ampthill

BENEATH THE SURFACE

They never knew me. No one decided to look beyond my silvery skin, instead decided to see a heartless monster. If they did, they would realise my undying pain. They would find my bleeding heart. It had been bleeding long before they decided to strike me with their deceptive gadgets. I bled with one wish; I wanted to make friends, swim amongst them. Parents tell their children to smile, make friends. One befriended me once. He was killed during our game. I will be reunited with him. Become a myth told to children. A myth of a deadly monster. Jaws.

Kate Robinson (14)
Redborne Upper School & Community College, Ampthill

EVIL

Evil. A word I hear daily. People preach kindness but when you dive into the deep rabbit hole of darkness you can't escape. I only did what I did to stay in the shadows. But everyone gets pushed enough eventually? No. I did what I did to survive society. This big world pressures people to feel so little. Save the planet! Save the planet! How can we do such a thing when we can't even save ourselves? Some of the purest hearts are allured to the darkness. Nothing you can prevent. Some people are just born evil.

Maizie Camfield (14)
Redborne Upper School & Community College, Ampthill

UNLIKELY TEAM

Why do they always send children?

"-defeat you!" the kid finished, hands shaking from... anger? Fear?

Limnox sighed. "Look, kid. I don't want to fight you."

He scoffed, drawing his (weakly) enchanted sword. "Of course not. You continue plaguing this land with magic," he replied, spitting. Ironic coming from the one with an enchanted sword.

"No, I don't want to fight a child. Despite what you've been told, I'm not a monster... At least, not to those who don't deserve it." She glanced at his sword before noting the kid's frankly atrocious stance. "Listen, kid. How about you and me...?"

Lucy Nicholson
Ridgeway Academy, Welwyn Garden City

WHAT'S HAPPENED TO ME...?

What am I doing? I approached five young children holding a knife, a smile grew on my face. After making that godforsaken deal with Glitchtrap, I could barely control myself. I grabbed one, Cassidy. Her cries for her parents got weaker. I stabbed her quickly, dropping her into a corner... I murdered them all, I'm a monster.

Years went by and I was the cornered one. Looking around, I grabbed my spring locked suit and rushed it on my skinny torso. I thought I escaped but I forgot it would malfunction with water. A click could kill me immediately. *Click*...

Claudia Costrasel
Ridgeway Academy, Welwyn Garden City

ALONE

Alone. Alone he stood in the night. He looked down on the blood-soaked, lifeless body, eyes staring endlessly up at the stars. His breathing was fast and shallow, his heart beating unsteadily as his knees became weak and hands started to shake uncontrollably. He tore his eyes from the ghastly sight to stare down at the knife in his hand, the dripping blood glistening in the moonlight.

"There! He did it! Get him!" a voice cried in the distance. Suddenly he realised what had happened, it had all been a blur, the anger, the blood, the silence. He killed him.

Daniel Stackman (14)

Ridgeway Academy, Welwyn Garden City

MY MOTHER KNEW BEST

I wish I was young. I wish I was pleasing. I've wished on every star but here I am! My years framed on my face through the darkness painted beneath my envious eyes, the silver strokes through my once soot-black hair. My mother said I was calamitous. Everywhere I went, I caused tribulation. But after all, my mother knew best. When those tyrants called me hideous, hoary, she knew to keep me inside, away. Here I shudder, the golden child perched in my arms. She shall rectify my future. Make me youthful. No more wishing. Let her power shine.

Codi Rowley-Connolly (13)
Ridgeway Academy, Welwyn Garden City

SCAR'S REDEMPTION

I had never belonged in the pride. I had never belonged anywhere. All that was given to me, my sanity, who I wanted to become, was deducted away from me. As I was thrown from Pride Rock, I felt anger surge through my body. Had I really let my guard down? Everything I did was to survive. Hyenas swarmed around me. Flames roared into the coal sky and immense heat tore at the scraps of my sun-kissed fur. Mufasa deserved his death but Simba... Simba deserves nothing. As I loiter in the outlands, planning vengeance, dark evil lurked within me.

Gracie Field (14)
Ridgeway Academy, Welwyn Garden City

JOKER FINDS A FRIEND

Have you heard of the Joker? A misunderstood man, lost in his own thoughts. A boy that had been abused at a young age. Burnt, hit, scarred. He was given the scars from his reckless father who had been drinking. He had been through psychological hell. He had been twisted by the society around him.

He found his sanctuary portraying his life upon the world, showing how they treated him. He had to find someone that goes through pain and make them think how they are mentally. He can use their pain, their torture, and make them like him.

Nathan Hill (14)
Ridgeway Academy, Welwyn Garden City

THESEUS AND THE MINOTAUR

Suddenly, there I was, a sword through my chest, my neck slashed and the next heir's foot on my chest with a beaming smile.

Everyone thought I was evil, I was a beast. Roaming around and protecting helpless creatures. Until the kingsmen found me, beat me, starved me, and after a week of pain and starvation, I was thrown into a labyrinth to be forgotten about.

There was no escape. The king sent down poor children for sacrifice. I was so desperate I ate them. The king sent more and more until I was slain. I finally found peace.

Roman Flack (13)
Ridgeway Academy, Welwyn Garden City

THE LION'S SHARE

I was told I was destined for immense greatness. Told I could rule the kingdom by my father. And despite being resourceful, I was banished. My hatred for my brother started when my father died, and a power struggle began. The question is, who would take over? It was a fierce fight. Many times, we saw Death, but as I always say - I had the lion's share of the brains, but he had the brawn. When he won, I was banished to plot my revenge. The death of my brother will be satisfying, but will they accept my amiable rule?

David James (14)
Ridgeway Academy, Welwyn Garden City

THE BOY WHO ONCE LIVED TO DREAM

It all began when I was a child. The demons had ravaged my village as children, mothers and fathers escaped for the safety of their lives. I was only an ordinary boy until I saw her, my mother, being devoured by a bloodthirsty demon. I wanted to do something, but I couldn't move. My body was engulfed by a raging flame of anger which would not be extinguished until I got my revenge. I couldn't defeat it though. I wasn't strong enough. So I have come back as an entity to haunt the one who killed my mother.

April Warwick (14)
Ridgeway Academy, Welwyn Garden City

WAS THAT ME?

Friday 13th

I cursed a naive beautiful, babbling baby. As I towered over the cot, thoughts tumbled through my mind; this was my revenge. Her mother loathed me and always had. She was terrified of my sleek, curved horns, jealous of my freeing unclipped wings. Her perpetual torment during school was degrading. Now my chance to show her pain, the pain I endured for 15 years. It's only an innocent child, however, the world is tough, and I regret it, but in the moment...

Saturday 14th

Suffering. Sorrow. Remorse.

Lucy Claridge (13)

Ridgeway Academy, Welwyn Garden City

PROMISES

What was I doing...? I approached the young children, but then a pain grew in my stomach. After what I promised to the witch I knew that I couldn't turn back. I gripped one of the young girls by their arm and put the knife to their neck, her cries grew louder. I killed each and every one of the children. I'm a monster, a beast.

Years later, I looked up at the sky with sorrow. I stood up in agony and walked towards the edge of a cliff. Slowly and carefully, stepping off, I fell to the ground...

Verity Rowe (13)
Ridgeway Academy, Welwyn Garden City

THE COMMON ENEMY

I have accepted the fact that I am fake. No matter how real I feel to me, I know that I was a concept made up by others to help them keep track of everything. I have no heart, no brain, no life. All I can do is move forward.

Some people say that I'm against them. But that is untrue. I am just a being, with no knowledge of love and hate, that was how they designed me. Yet still, they resent me.

They hate my unstoppable tick-tock as I move forward.

Ava-Mae Burlingham (14)

Ridgeway Academy, Welwyn Garden City

UNWANTED DOINGS

Who would've claimed such a shallow soul to be broken and or hurt? Not cruel with harsh intentions of taking the life of another, but instead aching to feel the touch of a humane soul. They want and need to feel a warm-blooded hand against his. A curse forced upon him; where the force to take life from another. He wishes to hold them tightly and apologise for his unwanted doings. As he hangs his head low, and a clutch on a crimson-dipped scythe, he weeps his sorrows to the one who brought this upon him... The people.

Emily
Rishworth School, Rishworth

DAY OFF

I seriously think that having a day off will do me good. You know, all the murdering is bad for my mental health. So I decided to have a day off. I woke up and went to the kitchen. I toasted some bread and reached for the jar of blood. I stopped myself. Maybe I should have jam for once. After that, I had a good old walk. I saw someone and reached for one of my many knives, but then I remembered, *I'm having a day off.* So I kept on walking. I sat down. What a good day!

Henry Kitson (11)
Rishworth School, Rishworth

THE TRUTH BEHIND QUEEN GRIMHILDE

It was hardly her fault. She had grown up thinking that beauty meant everything, because of the leaders that ruled The Ernsfield 100 years ago. Mr White was the leader at that time and if you were ugly, you were executed. Make-up did not exist in those times and so people were dying by every second. The clock was ticking. Grimhilde's mum was executed for apparently being ugly, according to Mrs White. It was purely Snow White's fault. She brought chaos. She was the sole reason that Grimhilde wanted to poison Snow White. That day was etched in Grimhilde's memory.

Jasleen Dhami (13)
Seva School, Coventry

VENOM

Once I was a 'nobody' but now I'm the most fearsome of entities. It all started when I was a photographer, working for the Daily Bugle. I was called Eddie Brock. Life was perfect until I met named Peter Parker came to ruin me. He seemed to be photographing that dastardly superhero, Spider-Man. He gave it to Jonah Jameson first. Was this a web of deceit? When I got an opportunity for greatness, Spider-Man showed up. His web straightjacketed me. They were clearly in cahoots. This happened many times until I got fired and lost everything. Then I became Venom.

Adithyan Athinarayanan (13)
Seva School, Coventry

THE LONELY QUEEN

Meandering through the forest I desperately hoped to see new life. Treading over sticks, accidentally planting my feet in mud, my cloak was torn, my hair tangled. I slipped my hood over my head. Glancing around my surroundings, a serene lady caught my eye. Quickly grabbing my woven basket full of ripe apples, I strode over to her. She greeted me warmly. I offered one of my hand-picked apples and she accepted it without any hesitation. She took the biggest bite. To my utter horror, she fell. I peered inside the apple; emerald liquid oozed menacingly. Who tricked me?

Laila Heer (12)
Seva School, Coventry

THE FOUR ELEMENTS

Jisoo was a girl. She had superpowers. Her friends had superpowers. Their names were Jennie, Lisa and Rose. Their powers were fire, earth, air and water. Jisoo had fire power. Jennie had earth power. Lisa had water power and Rose had air power. They were 'The Four Elements'. But of course the villain was there. The Four Elements were at school and someone started to destroy the city. When the girls heard and saw what happened in that time, The Four Elements went into their city to save their people from the villain. They saved the entire city.

Alexia Chis (12)
Seva School, Coventry

VOLDEMORT

One day during the new year, my grandma died. Two days before my birthday, my sister died. Tragedy upon tragedy struck me every day. Pleading for the hope of God, I prayed, fasted, and cried. Non-stop. I was comforted by my father. So sweet, so devious. He was a devil inside an angel. Lurking in the shadows. His penchant and thirst for blood were highly disgusting. I think he killed my grandma. I'm on an investigation. He transformed into a monster. He was black, had large teeth and was slimy. He left me with a trauma I'll never, ever forget.

Daniella Nsiouba (12)
Seva School, Coventry

FUTURE OF POSION IVY

My gruesome grandma dropped the bombshell that she was a villain. She was called Poison Ivy and she was going to pass her powers to me. I didn't want to be a dastardly villain! But I wanted to be a super-heroine. So I didn't tell her about my future plans. My granny told me to pass my powers to my kids. I promised and started plotting. I am now eighteen and I know how to control my powers. My grandma passed away a few weeks ago. Now, I can be a super-heroine. A superheroine who the world adores! I'm ecstatic!

Sanmeet Kaur (13)

Seva School, Coventry

THE OTHER SIDE

I exhaled, seeing a huge bulky man staring at my corpse, lying on the floor with blood splattered on the walls and across his balaclava.

It felt off at that moment.

It was as if my life was empty and just a big, black hole of emptiness. My heart ached, even though I had a gaping hole instead of a heart.

Staring at the crimson corpse, I realised I could either join forces with the Devil or rest in peace.

At that very moment, I knew I had a chance to unleash my dastardly dark side and go absolutely berserk.

Karam Singh Dhillon (12)
Seva School, Coventry

THE HESPERIDES

They're stunning, bodies carved from sunlight and voices wrought with the shining of the stars. The seven of them surround a breathtaking tree, from which hangs what appears to be golden fruit. They sing beautifully, warmly, sweetly and it's intoxicating and suddenly I can't breathe, the sound of their honeyed drawls enveloping me mercilessly. Then, suddenly, it ceases. I'm left craving the feeling of the melody in my ears, left yearning for the encasing sight of their smiles. I long so much it becomes painful, and in my hysteria, I don't register the wicked blades in their hands.

Morgan
Sir Frederick Gibberd College, Harlow

SKINWALKER

A sharp white complexion shone through the blackness of the midnight sky. As Codie stared into what seemed to be a never-ending black abyss, through the glass of his window, this possessed skinwalker lured outside night after night but just to disappear by sunrise. It all started when Codie heard someone screaming for help, just to be trapped in this skinwalker's path. The foul beast moved towards the window into the dim light, he could just barely make out the furry goat-like figure. The beast had been there every night for the past month before it attacked...

Hollie
Sir Frederick Gibberd College, Harlow

HADES

You may have heard of me; I'm Hades - the 'bad god'. This may shock you, but the 'heroes' are not really heroes. This started shortly after we defeated the Titans. Although I helped greatly, none of them cared about me, only about themselves. I was banished. Left alone. I only wanted to be loved, but they didn't love me, so I had to take matters into my own hands. I fell for their beloved Persephone. She's kind and incredibly beautiful. She provides all the company I need. I was never this happy before her. I truly love her.

Lily-Anne Holliland (13)
Sir Frederick Gibberd College, Harlow

GLIOBLASTOMA

I still haven't forgotten the day she was diagnosed with Glioblastoma. She arrived home and broke the news. I had to kill Tony Stark. He had the money that I needed to pay for my mother's medication. I trained to assassinate. Despite having paid for my mother's medication, she died. I couldn't comprehend the fact that she was gone. My dad wasn't around. He abandoned us... Me.

There's no point trying to redeem myself. It's all over the news. Everyone hates me anyway. Who cares if I get arrested or executed? It's time to have some fun!

Molly Loughran
St Anne's Primary School, Finaghy

THE DARKEST HOUR

Dear Reader,

Hi! My nickname is Sneak, and I am a child villain. My parents are also villains and they taught me how to steal without being caught or heard, hence the name. Anyway, we started becoming a villain family because, when I was five, this happened:

Screech! Shudder! My parents were asleep. Suddenly, out of nowhere, a bullet shot through my window. I screamed and tried to run but another bullet was fired, and it shot through my leg and I let a deafening howl of pain. My parents ran downstairs and looked out of the window. The killer.

Isabella Hirlemann-Garcia (12)
St Anselm's Catholic School, Canterbury

INSTINCT

Instinct. A fixed pattern of behaviour in animals. Tell me, if a creature simply followed its instinct to survive, would it be chastised for it? If I would have just left my 'victims' to live and thrive, I would be a rotting, malnourished corpse. Alas, I have been labelled a cold-blooded monster. You could say my methods do prove to petrify those who stand before me. But each whine, each yell, each cry? No matter the flesh bag, it all feels normal. And honestly? Each whimper of agony makes my lust for flesh even stronger.

Lara Thompson (14)
St Anselm's Catholic School, Canterbury

I'M COMING...

I've never really belonged. I found the gory details in 'horrible things' hilarious. I was hysterical when someone hurt themselves. Everyone hated me. They thought I was possessed. I had to find out. One day, I skipped school and went to a fortune-teller.

Yes, Phoenix, I know everything. How you possessed me as a baby, gave me a horrible name and an evil personality. I'm coming. You'll regret everything you've done to me. I'm now apparently the baddy because I want revenge. Wouldn't anyone? My life is ruined because of you. Am I wrong for wanting a normal life?

Molly Taylor (12)
St Dominic's Grammar School, Brewood

THE WINTER SOLDIER

"I am with you till the end of the line," I said confidently. I flashed back to reality, I remembered my mission. I had to kill Captain America. Stupidly, he dropped his shield. This was the moment to complete my assignment!
"Your name is James Buchanan Barnes," he said weakly. My head was racing. It was like my mind and body were fighting. It all came back to me. I was kidnapped by a Nazi organisation. Hydra. My best friend Steve is the Captain. Before I could do anything else, Steve murmured my signature line. He plunged into the water...

Aaron Puri (12)
St Dominic's Grammar School, Brewood

REVENGE!

I still haven't forgotten! On that fateful night when I crept into baby Potter's room he thwarted my attempt to take over the world. I underestimated the power of his magic and his desire to live. I still can't believe how a child defeated the greatest sorcerer to ever hold a wand. I will regenerate my physical body and mind to strike him down and wipe his memory off the face of the earth and let everyone know that I am the most dominant wizard of them all. Potter, never close your eyes I am coming for you! Revenge!

James Wesley (11)

St Dominic's Grammar School, Brewood

THE REAL VILLAIN!

You may know the tale of The Amazing Spider-Man and Electro, but have you ever imagined it from the so-called villain's perspective? From Electro's point of view, this is how it went: Spider-Man is a liar. He promised me he would come, but of course, he has better things to do than go to his biggest fan's birthday. I was invisible to everyone but not anymore. I have so much power. Then he lied again and let the police try and fail to kill me. Now that I have power, I will destroy him and everyone that he loves!

Tegh Singh Bahra (12)
St Dominic's Grammar School, Brewood

DRACO MALFOY

I never really belonged at Hogwarts. Anyone I had ever known had either abandoned me or died. I was left alone. My father never really loved me. Potter got everything. Everything I had earned had got handed to *him*. I think I know what I need to do. I need to kill Harry Potter. I really don't want to but I have no choice. I adore Hermione but I fear if I kill her best friend, she will envy me until I die. Potter, if you are reading this, I'm coming for you. Sleep with one eye open tonight.

Harleen Bains (12)
St Dominic's Grammar School, Brewood

BECOMING BAD

I never really belonged in my family. My mom, dad, sister and I were superheroes, but just after my mom died everything changed. My dad started to go out of the house a lot and every time he came back, a crime had just been committed. Months later, he never returned; it was just me and my sister. We got placed into care and that's when I met my friend, Tom. We started to go out of the house a lot and do things we weren't meant to. But this time is my time for revenge. Watch out, Dad...

Isabelle Richards (11)

St Dominic's Grammar School, Brewood

THE ANTLERS

The sky was clear, showing an ominous glowing circle above. Below they gathered. The Antlers. They were covered in leaves like walking bushes. These creatures were almost human but had antlers. This is what gave them their name. They hunt down travellers who enter their territory and steal their souls for energy. The biggest, the leader, stepped forward and looked around. "I sense a human."
"We haven't eaten for a month," another said.
Suddenly, a net fell down. The leader and the others stared. A human stepped out from the bushes. "No more hunting!"
"But we only hunt to survive."

Cohen Williams (12)
Sutton Academy, St Helens

THE HIDDEN SECRET

Eleven-year-old Evan had been missing and presumed dead for two years. His older brother Michael, a policeman, had vowed to find out what happened to him. Michael sat with Evan's best friend Lucas in the cafe staring at the Fredbear robot. Michael knew something was bothering Lucas. Suddenly, the Fredbear made a noise, it sounded like Evan's voice. Lucas jumped up as did Michael. They crept over to Fredbear and it was Evan's voice.

"Lucas, why did you kill me?" said Fredbear, quietly. Michael froze. Suddenly he realised that his brother's killer... was standing right next to him!

Ethan Dyer (11)
Sutton Academy, St Helens

THE CRACKLER: REDEEMING MY TRUTH

That fallacious hero was an erroneous freak. The mendacious *Night-Saviour* got his fans by misleading acts. I rescued their pathetic lives from bio-devouring dangers whilst he created them. Yet, they thought I was the cruel evil-doer: they called me the *Crackler*. His wild fans tried to cause chaos towards me. They tried to attack me, humiliate me and taunt me. I went through a tough time until I met Arch-Redeemer. He promised to help me get The Night-Saviour. It was time we reveal the false hero. With the help of the *Arch-Redeemer*, Saviour's true acts were delivered to the police.

Saleem Abdulaleem (12)

Sutton Academy, St Helens

THE INVASION OF THE INFECTED SAILORS

One placid evening, sailors were about to set sail to try and find samples of new unexpected species. The captain of the ship sat down and sipped a drink, just as the waters were enraged and became turbulent. The acquiescent sailors obeyed every command of the captain. As the sea became rougher, a green glowing substance covered the entire ship and seemed to seep through the gaps around the windows. The second in command managed to get a sample. It seemed to be infected, but just before he turned the crew had instantly been infected. It's just the beginning...

Tyler Lawrenson (12)

Sutton Academy, St Helens

SWEET PRINCESS

I cursed the king's child, that she'd prick her finger on a spinning wheel on her sixteenth birthday. As I went back to the moors, I laughed in the face of death. That sweet princess would be no more. I woke up to a strange sound. The king was in the moors, searching for an antidote for the princess. Furiously, I decided he would pay for this! The sound drew closer. I wrapped my vines tight around his neck, draining all life. He was gone. When I got to the castle, the princess was sleeping... Soon for a long time.

Zara Honey (11)
Sutton Academy, St Helens

THE BIG BAD WOLF

I never really belonged in the village with everyone else. I was different. I had wolf-like features and instincts. Everybody always laughed and pointed at me. They were so scared of me. I knew I had to do one thing. The forest was the only place I had freedom. My life was now ruining other people's lives. I wanted to take revenge for what they had done to me! My plan worked, I had manipulated my prey. I was going to eat her grandma and then eat her after. I knew that it was wrong, but I couldn't stop myself...

Gemma Wood (12)

Sutton Academy, St Helens

THE MONSTER NEXT DOOR

It was a dark and misty night and no one was in sight. Mike came out of his house to take the bins out when he heard a rustling just behind the bush. He pulled out his phone and switched the torch on. He had a split second of life and *wham!* Dead...

The next morning his neighbour Jill came to check on him, and she saw his body just outside his front door. Next second Mike's head ripped off his neck and spider-like legs came out of his temples and his monstrous head chased Jill until the end...

Oscar Ballard (11)
Sutton Academy, St Helens

THE SUPERNATURAL WORLD

In reality, I'm the good guy and he's the bad guy. I snuck back into the town square, the world was in my palm until he came into this world. All I knew was that I was coming back. I had to think of something malicious, evil, one of a kind. My backstory was the past, this is the future, the vicious future. I'll create an army and ruin him, his people and the town square. I might be as scaly as a snake or as hairy as a Gruffalo but I'll never let him defeat me. I'm a winner.

Aksheka Varathes (11)

Sutton Academy, St Helens

THE NIGHT THAT CHANGED HIS LIFE

1932

It was a dark and stormy night, you could hear stray dogs howling through the pitch-black sky. James and his parents walked through a creepy alleyway to go home. But on the way was a man. Dark and shadowy, he came up and shot both parents, then ran off into the dark. James never could have imagined that this day would change his life forever...

1952

Twenty years later, James runs into a bank. Wielding a gun, he demands all of their money.

Kai Pan (12)

Sutton Academy, St Helens

VILLAINY IS HARD!

I'm Rob, the self-appointed world's greatest supervillain. You'd think being a villain is easy, but if you want to be legit there's a whole lot more to it. First, decide who to rob, and how, accounting for security/police. The next important step is lunch, before gathering equipment and a team. Here comes my favourite part, the one with all the action... coffee break. Then there's the robbery, blah blah, share out the riches, blah blah, and crucially, dinner. Now you know how tough being a villain is, here's one last essential tip - never ever trust a clown.

Joey Selsick (12)
The Archer Academy, East Finchley

AGONAL

Those tallies, that ledger, it means nothing. Claim that last gasp. All those with consciousness will eventually meet me. They accuse me of extinguishing lives too young, of being a monster; I know better. The universe needs me. Without me, the scales become unbalanced, chaos will fall upon this plane. On their knees, they beg. Mercy. I simply can't be held responsible. I'm not the one who killed them. I've never taken a life in my entire existence. I am simply a guide for the souls that were taken by the cruellest, most monstrous being of them all: life.

Freya McLaughlin
The Carlton Academy, Carlton

MOTHER...

There they were; brother and sister, in a forest. They took the path unknown. Crumbs left to find their way home. After what seemed an eternity, they found shelter. A house that was good enough to eat: every little child's dream. With an abrupt push of the door, it swiftly swung open, and with a swish of a cloak, there she was: Mother.
"Double, double, toil and trouble; fire burn and cauldrons bubble." Into the house the children went, into the cauldron they flew, and out of the cauldron their skeletons blew. The witch cackled with glee. They were dead...

Hani Alachkar (12)
The Literacy House International, Tintagel

THE CHOICE

I did it to survive. It was my only choice. I had wanted to live, and I needed a soul. She was my choice, such a pretty little flower, cursed to take her life for me to live. She looked like her, which I loathed. Such an innocent face, the face must go. I killed two birds with one stone, removing her from my life and getting what I need. But… was it worth the guilt I am feeling now? If she were alive, would I want to do this? Now, the sweet silence of death…

Hannah Lee-Parry (15)
The Literacy House International, Tintagel

THE GOLDEN HARP

He was the one who started it. I only attacked him to defend myself. He was the one who broke into my home and stole my goose and harp, my source of income and the only thing that was keeping me fed. I only chased him and tried to kill him because he was stealing from me while I was sleeping. He thought that just because I was living in a castle on the top of a cloud, I would be rich. But all I had was those two prized possessions from my family.

Ian Lee-Parry (15)
The Literacy House International, Tintagel

ZOMBIE ATTACK

Dan and Rose had three horses called Jamie, Pixie and Momo. They also had a beautiful foal called Rosie. Rosie became ill and needed a vet. Dan called the vet. When he came, he seemed really nice, his name was Mr Putin. Dan went to make him a cuppa, whilst Mr Putin looked at the horse. On Dan's return, Mr Putin had vanished. Rosie began to turn into a zombie! She had turned the whole world into zombies. Who could save us all now? Can we find Mr Putin?

Corey Claypole (12)
The Old School House, Friday Bridge

I DIDN'T HAVE A CHOICE, OURS IS NOT TO REASON WHY

It was do or die. These... things, they kill everything in sight. The Dilophosaurus spat its venom, scorching the trees behind; the scent of burnt wood and flesh from my fallen allies reached my nostrils, making me gag. I knew it was a living creature with a family and feelings, but it was either me or the dinosaur. I raised my dead comrade's M16A1, glued my eyes shut and unloaded the magazine. It felt like a knife plunged into my gut as I heard it cry out in agony, before a sickening thud. It was over. I had survived.

Alejandro Peñart-Buck (11)
The Peterborough School, Peterborough

PATHIC

Victoria Vanderson was having a day off from planning her next victim's demise. Victoria is a particularly interesting girl. As a psychopath she plots and plans every aspect of her life down to the finest detail but, on this day, she decided not to plan anything at all. Instead, she phoned her therapist 'friend' who she always anonymously calls. On this day she asks him something that's been on her mind, "Would I still be so bad if I had empathy?"
"Of course you would," he laughed.
"Would I?"

Aaron Pearce (13)

The Quay School, Parkstone

CANNIBAL

It haunted her mind. The screams and the begging of the people she murdered and ate prior. But now, now she was dragging her sharp knife through the flesh. There was nothing it could do to stop her. She ripped the legs off and cut open the stomach as the blood covered her hands, reaching into the stomach and harvesting out the organs and throwing them to the side. Humming a sweet song, she got all the body parts and lay them on a tray. Once cooked, she called down her children to let them know the chicken was cooked.

Gracie-Marie Hall (13)
The Quay School, Parkstone

THE FORSAKEN WOLVES

The cheering crowds, the chanting from the candlelit town hall, that is what the attackers could hear. They eyed the town for cattle. A failure in catching the livestock would endanger the whole pack. They'd spotted their prey, just waiting to be caught. They began their attack. At first, no one heard them. Eight wolves advanced toward their prey. Abruptly, cries of a wolf distracted the rest of the pack. A human towered over with his bloodstained axe. The alpha gazed, traumatised at the sight of his son's body. He fled into the doomed countryside where all wolves became extinct.

Ben Culbard (12)
The Redhill Academy, Arnold

THE JOKER'S SECRETS

I still haven't forgotten the day it all occurred, in Gotham City. The day my life changed forever. I just want to be free. I'm trapped in my own body, but I'm not alone. I bury my complications beneath my face paint. I do it to survive, not only to save myself but my family too. My deck of cards remedy the anxious voices in my muddled head. However, if you dive deeper into the pack, my true colours start to show. Something is devouring me. Slowly. Venturing through me until it's too late.

Harry Williams (12)
The Redhill Academy, Arnold

NOT GUILTY

How do I plead? Not guilty of course! Why would I feel guilty for something I didn't do? I'm just a simple boy, who wants to learn. I wasn't the one that threw a table out the window! Oh, I didn't know she needed glasses. What happened that day? We were on a trip, see, to this really interesting cliff-side. It was used in the ninth century, as a... Oh, sorry. My teacher went for a smoke. All I did was tap her on the shoulder. I didn't push her. It was the wind. So, I plead not guilty.

Joseph Hempshall (14)

The St Leonards Academy, St Leonards-On-Sea

THE THINGS THEY MAKE ME DO

Staring down at my shaking hand, I saw the knife dripping warm, crimson blood. *Oh God, no, please not him too.* I hate them; how they get into your head, make you do things you would never do, and hurt people you would never dream of hurting, people you love. Thunder crashed outside, and the dim yellow lights flickered. The rain was pattering on the roof lightly as if it was whispering. Dread washed over me. He was all I had left; I am alone now. I can't face them alone.

Maya Houghton (13)
The St Leonards Academy, St Leonards-On-Sea

THE PIPER'S SON

The crimson substance slithered off my golden blade chiselled with black roses. My dagger illuminated their cold, motionless bodies with an eerie maroon glow. I didn't mean to do these atrocious acts that made my stomach churn at the thought of them. They were threatening my family. I, the piper's son, whose only purpose is to vaporise their sins. I, the piper's son, a child with his life demolished. I, the piper's son, am the villain of this story. I, the piper's son, who can only play one bloody and sinful melody. Death. Such a simple word for something colossal.

Nico Gesner
The Stanway School, Stanway

A LITTLE BIRDIE TOLD ME I WAS DEAD

Day and night, I sit here isolated in my tiny pitch-black room staring and gazing, admiring my past friends' sorrow and sadness. Watching them through distorted, blurry cameras enjoy every second of life with not a thought that they destroyed mine. They told me that I was a horrendous, sinful creature yet they transformed me into this. I used to be carefree and gleeful. I would sing along to the tune of the birds and laugh over every mistake. They crippled that though, tore my self-esteem and crumbled my happiness. I want revenge and when I want, I receive.

Samiya Barker (12)
The Stanway School, Stanway

THE REAL JOKER

Footsteps echo in the distance. He follows me everywhere. All I see is a figure that disappears in a blink of an eye when I turn around. I look like I enjoy being destructive. I don't. People call me the devil. It's all a lie. He controls me. Frames me. Voices scream in my head so loud I can't hear my thoughts. He's going to catch me someday. He's getting closer. I'm a trapped bird in a cage. Under this smile of wickedness hides the real me. I'm the Joker, I don't want to be malevolent. He's the real villain...

Lucy Arbuckle
The Stanway School, Stanway

THE BREAK-IN

The night of the break-in, wearing black clothes and comfortable sneakers, I made it to the laboratory. Ten blocks away in only six minutes. I circled the building and found a slightly open window, so climbed up into a bathroom, it had an open door. I found the machine on floor twenty-two. I transported the machine. It was a lot smaller than I first thought. After searching almost all the floors I found him on the fifth, just doing some work.

"I can bring you in awake and with no bruises or the hard way."

Finley Marchant (13)

The Stanway School, Stanway

THE BLACK DEATH

I did it for the heart of the land. The destructive creatures only care for themselves. Only think for themselves. Every time one is born, a new crack is created in the earth. When there were few of them, they noticed how we acted and followed. Now, there are billions and they only do what they want for pleasure. I let rats do the dirty work. They tried to exterminate them all... They failed. I was the death of lots but not all. I fought for our land that wasn't theirs. I failed... Is there any way to defeat them?

Indy Turpin (12)

The Stanway School, Stanway

IMPERFECTIONS

How was I supposed to know this would happen? I never meant for anyone to die. Oh well. Not everyone can be perfect. Least of all little old me who was always just tagging along. Watching. Waiting. But no one ever questioned it, they didn't even hear me out and look where that got us. Now she sits up there all high and mighty as if her throne isn't made out of all of those she stood on to get it. How could she so willingly leave everything behind, leave us behind? It was all fake. I hope she crumbles.

K Fierce (15)

Torlands Academy, St Thomas

THE DINING ROOM

I strode into a small, dull cave. I pressed my arm against the back of it revealing a gap I could squeeze through. Lit candles revealed a dining table around which sat four people I recognised as family. My silent family with their stiff postures. Their skin matched the stone of the walls with green and purple patches. Their eyes were vacant, and their hands clearly outlined each of the bones inside. Their abdomens were so thin that their skin could easily tear from their ribcages. However, nothing would distract me from dinner with the perfect family I had created.

Michael Stafford
Truro & Penwith College, Truro

LETTER TO THE LIVING

Sometimes I'm the villain. Sometimes not so much. Fate isn't written by me; you're the author. Each one is nameless to me: a mother, father, brother, sister... The less I know, the better. I string the souls up, my own constellation in the firmament. A map of icy sapphires lighting up the dark in the suburbs of the unknown. I haven't taken them, stolen them from you. I've only placed them a little further from reach for all to see. A gallery of loss. A museum of memories. So call me a villain if it makes you feel better. -Death.

Maddy Vincent (17)
Truro & Penwith College, Truro

THE TRUTH ABOUT 1985

Finally, I have done it; I have given my partner a bad name and a rotten body. I wanted to go home but guilt stopped me. How could a father be a criminal? Father. That single word reminded me of the empty hole in my chest. My family... all gone. Because of him... I looked at the lifeless body and my tattered grey suit, wet and bloodstained. It was his fault the engineering went wrong. His fault they died. The suit then collapsed in on me, crushing my body and making the floor red. I screamed but nobody came. "Henry!"

Siddhartha Sharma Adhikari (11)
Upton Court Grammar School, Slough

VICTORIOUS VILLAINS

Finally, I was about to win. After all those years of stealing, I was going to get it. *Bang!* Captain Leo broke through the window.

"What do you want?" I shouted.

"I have come to arrest you!"

"What? Ugh... Why?" I shouted.

"You have stolen something," he said.

"What? No, I haven't."

"I don't believe you," he said, grabbing a rope and tying me up.

"No, let me out of here!" Captain Leo grabbed the jewellery, putting it back on the shelves.

"No!" Captain Leo arrested me. I grabbed his neck and strangled him. *Yes! I am finally free!*

Anayah Quddous (12)
Westholme School, Blackburn

WHO'S THE REAL VILLAIN?

Poof! I watched as Captain Justice broke through the cloud I was chilling on.

"Ugh, what do you want now?" He looked at me, smirking.

"You're under arrest." I was shocked. I hadn't committed any crimes recently, so he was obviously lying.

"Sure, what have I done this time?" He pulled the Sapphire Elixir, the most valuable jewel around. I was shocked. "What the hell... You're framing me!"

Captain justice just smiled and said, "Who are they going to believe? The city hero or the villain famous for stealing?" I was about to fly away, but something strange stopped me...

Elizabeth Judah (12)
Westholme School, Blackburn

WHO'S THE REAL VILLAIN?

I was sitting, plotting in my lair, when the door exploded open. Rubble went flying everywhere. In the doorway stood my arch-nemesis, Dr Steel.
"Hello, Spectrum." He then handed me a big wad of cash. "So are things good?" He had a big smirk on his face.
Then reality hit me. "You robbed a bank, didn't you? To frame me!" I switched the television on and it said there had been a bank robbery last night! "It was you!" I exclaimed.
"Very clever, Spectrum. But who are they going to believe? Me, their hero, or you, their most wanted criminal?"

Jack Valentine (12)
Westholme School, Blackburn

BEHIND THE SCENES

Finally, my plan was in action. Everyone awoke, I'd been planning this for years. The government had implemented a mandatory law. Every citizen had to have a microchip in their brain. They called it the 'technological revolution'. They didn't realise there was a flaw. After an hour, I would finally be in control of everyone. I would finally get my revenge. People started getting used to the chips and started downloading data to their brains... I had almost gained access to the chips and everyone's brains, then an error occurred and I realised, someone had beaten me to it.

Sanad Saidan (14)
Westholme School, Blackburn

THUNDER PROOF

I was strolling behind Captain Thunder Stroke as he come back to Rivendell City to capture criminals. He seemed like he was very tired, so I decided that this was my chance. My chance to get revenge.

"Well, it was nice knowing you." He looked at me where I was. I was wearing rubber gloves and a rubber vest because they are 'thunder' proof.

"Where did you come from?" he said, very surprised. I quickly hit him straight in the head with my bat and tied him up with a rubber rope, his weakness.

"Well, that's definitely over," I laughed.

Esa Iqbal (12)
Westholme School, Blackburn

THE EVIL TEACHER

I still haven't forgotten... the teacher who'd poisoned her school students. She seemed like she cared but was a monster. Her students grew closer to her but it was an act. "Who wants water?" she asked students who were extremely hot. She handed out cups while dropping poison into each glass. The poison killed them... She dragged their lifeless bodies into a van and drove home to dismember each child. Laughing, she came up with an idea to try and bring her dead mother back with the organs of school children.
"Child soup sounds nice too."

Zaeemah Ali (14)
Westholme School, Blackburn

BEHIND THE SCENES

Finally, my plan was in motion. The drafts were completed. The models, ready to cause the utmost destruction. My desire was almost fulfilled. The faint sound of gentle whirring met my ears, and I hurried to peer out of my opaque windows, eager to see the chaos I willingly created. A sleek, shining white car smoothly slunk out of the opposite red-brick driveway, a contented passenger safely inside. Or so they thought. Within a millisecond, the car jolted into the tall trees beside the house, sending the car flying across the dry grass, upturning it. Now Steve Jobs would pay.

Olivia Ko (13)
Westholme School, Blackburn

THE FAILED PLAN

As my world blacked out I only saw that grinning face... I stood up. What had happened? Where was I? I'd had Vortex in my grip, the knife in my hand, ready to end the hero's life. Where was she? Where was her lifeless body? Why was the pentagram surrounding me? Why was the sky red? Where was the moon?

"No more questions my dear sinner," said a voice. I jolted to the right, there was a figure, cane in hand, top hat and a wicked grin.

"Welcome to hell, sinner, or should I say, villain. We've been waiting."

Jacob Cronshaw (11)
Westholme School, Blackburn

COLLECTING

Bobby the evil tax collector was counting his money, and so far he'd collected about £11,567,600. He now owned five cars, three mansions, and the whole of Japan. He was about to finish talking to his client on the phone. Suddenly the sidewall of his house blew up. In came a gigantic robot with a gigantic sucker on its arm.
"This is a lot of pounds, though it is not as much as I own," said Timmy, the really nice tax collector. He then sucked all of the money and left, leaving a really infuriated Bobby, desiring revenge.

Amaan Iqbal (14)
Westholme School, Blackburn

WHO'S THE REAL VILLAIN?

Fireboy was sat plotting a bank robbery when he spotted his bait. Fireboy walked slowly to the bank. He saw his bait cashing out money. He set off the alarm, shut down all the cameras and stole money. Fireboy saw his bait running and placed blame on him. He told his bait, "Are they going to believe you or me? The superhero." In the bait's head, he knew he didn't steal any money but he had money with him and no proof. So, the bait went to jail. Fireboy thought he was fine but he didn't know what was coming.

Farhan Dudhiya (12)
Westholme School, Blackburn

190

VICTORIOUS VILLAIN

Finally, I was about to win. After so many attempts, I was about to win world domination. All I had to do was blast the gun at the so-called hero, Captain Roberto. I started to think of all the glory and fame I would have. Dreams of swimming in gold would be mine...

Oh no, the scoundrel got away but I used my skill to corner him. I then asked him whilst holding the gun at him

"Any last words?" I then took one breath and said, "Hasta la vista."

Bang! Bang! Bang! Dead. Finished. I won.

Ismael Karolia (12)
Westholme School, Blackburn

VILLAIN MOTIVATION

That good girl act was all a lie. All these years, I'd had enough of her manipulating the teachers to congratulate her when she's done no good. I had a plan. A plan to end the favouritism. It was going to be over. She has no idea what I'm capable of. My plan was in motion, she was the first in class, as usual. I muttered, "Goodbye, evil one." I ran into the room, stabbing the knife into her neck. I looked down and realised I had made a huge mistake. I have to make up for what I've done.

Francesca Iles (14)
Westholme School, Blackburn

ORIGIN STORY

It's painful, betrayed by my sister. You see I really have the, well, what you might call a 'villain backstory'. I mean I found it quite difficult when I lost my parents: a fire, an apartment fire to be specific. Now back to my sister, she was the only one. We were there for each other, so much so we were inseparable. But that quickly changed. What still pains me is that she was with someone familiar, like I'd met them before. I only saw them for a quick amount of time. Who were they? I had to know.

Sophie Holt (12)
Westholme School, Blackburn

A SCAM

The beeping of the heart rate monitor constantly rang in the back of my head. I had to do something, even if it was drastic. After all, my child was terminally ill. But there was one more problem, I couldn't afford the hospital bills. I had a perfect idea, I had to become a scammer. I had to pretend to become a Nigerian prince and scam people. It was all for my son, Gideon. Over the next week, I worked tirelessly to get the money, scam after scam, but it was too late... My son had died during an operation.

Harry Gallery (13)
Westholme School, Blackburn

WHO'S THE REAL VILLAIN?

The superhero act was all a lie and I was about to be discovered, the 'enemy' was dead. Now, how was I supposed to show my resentment for the human race? I looked down at the small child clinging to my leg, the hate overtook me. This little child destroyed my planet along with the other people who now choose to applaud me and yet I save their lives? I will help them no longer. I lifted the child into the air and threw him towards the ground which showed everyone that I will no longer be their saviour.

Maia Lewis (13)
Westholme School, Blackburn

VICTORIOUS VILLAIN

Finally, I was about to win. I was staring at him with a ferocious grin, ready to make the final blow to end it all. He was pleading and begging for mercy, then he told me something that knocked my socks off. He told me where the most powerful item in the world was. The item that is my past, present and future. It was irresistible, letting him go, but I will do what I had to to get the prize. He told me it was in the vast mountains of Bavacado. I flung him into a cell and left.

A.Akitha Silva (11)
Westholme School, Blackburn

FEAR

Lying in bed that night, I could only be reminded of what was to come the next day. Waking up that morning gave me chills. It was time to face my fears. The first steps out the door onto my porch and off I went. Arriving at the destination, I could only be prepared for the worst. I sat waiting in silence for a couple of moments. But who or what is my fear? That's for me to know and for the world to find out.

Annabelle Waller (13)
Westholme School, Blackburn

I WILL HAUNT YOU

I just got out of jail for murder. The victim killed all my family. I had to hunt him down for payback. Life in jail wouldn't have been enough. I waited until the police came to the scene and I confessed. Now I haunt people in their sleep. When they see me, they scream and cry, they run to their mum and dads. In one kid's dream, he wasn't scared of me so I went to his house and scared him. He still wasn't scared, so I killed him in his room. I left him hanging from the roof.

Sonny Buckley (13)
Wickford Alternative Provision, Wickford

THE BIG BAD WOLF NEEDS REDEMPTION

Why must life be so cruel to wolves? It's common knowledge that if you encounter a wolf you'll meet your demise. Wolves are naturally ravenous so it's brutal to punish them. I'm getting blamed for evolution. It's not wolves who are barbaric, it's humans. Humans are destroying forests that wolves live in, making me find food elsewhere. They also have dogs that aren't that different from wolves but when dogs find something to eat they get praise. I'm not saying what I did was right but I had no choice. I'm being punished for merely surviving.

Sofia Spisakova (12)
Wingfield Academy, Rotherham

THE HOODED MAN

David was having a day off work so he decided to go online for some fun. However, he didn't know that something twisted was going to happen.

"Hey, what's your name? I'm David..."

No response.

"Oh, well, I'm 21 years old..."

"David, by any chance do you live at 38 Hill Road in Cumbria?" said a deep voice from somewhere.

"What, how do you know that? Go away, freak!"

As David panicked, he realised he couldn't leave. Then a man popped up, a hood over his head. David quickly closed his computer but when he did... there was a knock...

Sophie Irving (12)
Workington Academy, Workington

HORSING AROUND

Behind the scenes our plan was motivation. Me, Leona, Lexi and Hayden were on a mission to get revenge on their arch-nemesis. She was called Blondy. All of us were planning a master plan to destroy her. She needed to after what she had done. Lexi grinned, "I know exactly what to do," Leona laughed with pleasure.

"Go on."

"We can all watch her tonight and when it's the right time we pounce and Hayden can use her strength to throw her into the air. Kobie can use her mind powers and make Blondy turn to dust!"

Goodbye Blondy...

Kobie Metherell (13)
Workington Academy, Workington

HOW THE GRINCH STOLE THE HEART

His plan was in motion. The clock struck midnight. He sprung out of his chair in his lair and pranced to his steps. He frolicked up his stairs in the most absurd way. Exiting his mysterious hideout, he set off into the woods. He stood facing the forest, questioning whether he should go inside. He did. He stomped on top of the moss-filled branches and his phone spoke: "You have reached your destination." He immediately grasped his phone and repeatedly hit the phone until it stopped speaking. He dug into the ground and pulled out a Whos heart.

Lexi Williamson (13)
Workington Academy, Workington

THE BIG BATTLE

My plan was in motion, I was in my base underneath the barbers in Workington, getting ready to destroy Elizabeth.
"Come out, come out wherever you are." I had to get her to base as I had a surprise for her.
"I'm here Corey, and I have come prepared," Elizabeth explained.
"Well, you will have to get past me!" I said enraged by her.
I struck for a punch and so did she but I got there first. She was out cold so I brought her down to my base and she was imprisoned.
Now we are under control...

Reece Sowerby (12)
Workington Academy, Workington

THE VAMPIRE GIRL

"I can't believe she's gone..."
Flashback: It all started when I had to move somewhere else with my 'parents'. I did not want to move and I definitely did not like the house. It was small and cold. I had moved here twenty days ago. I kept sneaking out every night. I went into a forest that I did not know had werewolves in; I have a fear of werewolves. One came running towards me wagging its tail. I then felt the urge to kill people, It felt good. Then there were missing posters everywhere I went in different towns.

Olivia Conyers (12)
Workington Academy, Workington

TWISTED MISSION

I have been trusted. I can't let anybody down. I have to accept it. He was there already waiting for me. There was a long silence. My brother magicked a weird spell and at that moment, I heard the scream of my mother and children, the people I love the most in this world. My brother slowly turned around. "I have made a terrible mistake," and the next thing I knew, a fight was taking place. My brother had seriously injured himself and then he said his final words: "Goodbye, brother." I always still wonder, how did he know?

Hollie Gallacher (13)
Workington Academy, Workington

THE END OF MY JOB

As it stood, my job was safe. Joao Pedro and Joshua King had put my Watford side into the lead. I put our tactics to very defensive and the players sat back defending for their lives. However, Cristiano Ronaldo was there to ruin my Football Manager 2022 dreams by scoring two before half-time. Was my job finally over? I couldn't think about that. I told my players what I needed from them and how they could halt the board from terminating my contract. It was full time. Ronaldo scored three more. It was all his fault. He was the villain!

Cameron-John Allison (13)
Workington Academy, Workington

HUNTER

I still haven't forgotten. That day was the 20th June 1821. Why do I remember this? Because that was the day I died. You see, I've been alive for 200 years. You also might wonder why? Because I'm a vampire. And it's my turn to get revenge on the hunters who killed me. After years of searching, I've finally found them. I'm going to put them through the worst pain they ever experienced. I am going to kill them one by one so that no member of the hunters will ever walk the earth again. Finally, I'm going to win.

Hayden Turpin (12)
Workington Academy, Workington

JUST MONIKA

The lovely girl in a group of four starts to get jealous of the other girls... Suddenly one of the girls kills themselves and leaves three more girls in the club. The next girl turns insane. She stabs herself and passes away and then there are two girls left. It's only a matter of time before Monika deletes her file. Then there is just Monika. She sits with you, staring into your eyes, taking control over you. When you finally delete her, the game breaks down. Then you realise she's gone and she leaves you alone in the game.

Madison Robinson (13)
Workington Academy, Workington

INNOCENT

I had to make up for what I had done. I couldn't remember it but I'd killed her. I killed my best friend. We were drunk, so drunk I couldn't remember anything about it. I'd been locked up for months, waiting to go to court. The police had video evidence of us fighting but just after she screamed the video stopped. Nothing after that. I had bruises after our fight in the bar, I would be charged with murder. I knew it. Suddenly a policeman walked in. I was getting released. Her own mother had killed her and blamed me.

Holly Bennett (13)
Workington Academy, Workington

I MISS MY DAD

I still haven't forgotten when my dad left me in the woods. But I've finally got the courage to come back. I'm walking through when I step on something. It lets out a whimper and the next thing I know, I'm on the floor with a hand over my mouth. I can barely see. "Hello little girl," the man whispers. A huge grin spreads across his face. I try to scream but he dunks my head into the lake. "Mwahaha!" he screams. I am struggling to get up but then it stops. I gasp for air. There he is... Dad!

Scarlett Olvanhill (12)
Workington Academy, Workington

THE MOMENT I REALISED...

I didn't do it, no one believed me but I didn't. I don't know who did, helpful right? But I know I didn't. The only problem was, I was locked up in this house. Guards at every exit, no way out, no way to prove my innocence, no way to find who set me up or why they did it. I was a nobody; Alaina Woods, no friends, no enemies. Why would someone set me up? I haven't said anything to anyone, haven't done anything. I don't understand. Then I got the letter, everything fell into place. It was them...

Neve Stephens (13)

Workington Academy, Workington

THE SLEEPOVER

We were just sat there watching a movie when Scarlett put a crystal and some soot out of the fireplace on Sophie's head and we all thought nothing of it until we went to sleep. All of a sudden, as Scarlett told Sophie to be quiet, she opened her eyes and Sophie was floating up towards the ceiling. We both screamed as she grasped the roof. She started crawling all over it and then she opened her mouth and a bat flew out of it. She spoke, "Thank you for letting me out!" as she crawled up the fireplace.

Jaydan Knowles (13)
Workington Academy, Workington

JOKER'S SURPRISE

I still have never forgotten the day it all happened. It was a haunting Thursday night, the streets were empty. There was a blanket of clouds in the endless sky. It was pitch black. I'd just finished my work shift. Finally, what felt like a never-ending day had ended. I jumped on the sofa to watch a horror movie. Suddenly, the TV went static and would not work. A man with white face paint and green hair popped up and made a shiver roll down my spine. He jumped out and ripped my teeth out then disappeared.

Jacob Allison (12)
Workington Academy, Workington

THE SPIDER

You may not know me but to me you are an old friend. I know your business, your connections, your money. I know your whole life and you have no idea. They call me the spider. Crawling along the walls like terror in the night, or day. I come whenever I please... Once I'm done with you I go home, trade your information to the highest pleading bidder. Then that bidder buys you out of your precious clubs. I will crush you. Brick by brick your empire will crumble and you'll have no idea that it was me.

Scarlett Edmondson (13)

Workington Academy, Workington

THE MILK MONSTER

I did it to survive, waiting a week for him to come. Finally, I stepped into the haunted house. I lurked behind him and swiped. Missed! He started running, locking himself in a room. I found a way in. I always did. He turned and saw me. He saw I was made of milk and screamed. He was lactose intolerant. I went down his mouth, attacking his blood cells and veins. I slashed his heart and took his hair off. I left his body and watched him turn from red to blue to purple to white. Then he dropped dead.

Bailey Musgrave (13)
Workington Academy, Workington

MISS DENDY VS ME

I still haven't forgotten that day when I was pushed over in form. Even though I could not help being on the floor she still blamed me for being pushed over, disgusting. She saw everything that happened and was mad at me. She didn't even ask if I was okay after hitting my head on the table, wooden board around the plugs and the rock-solid floor. I was so angry at her for being pure evil to me and blaming me. Everyone else that saw it said it wasn't my fault. I will never forget.

Jamie Stoddart (13)
Workington Academy, Workington

BIG BAD MONSTER

I didn't mean to hurt them. I stay out of the way as I know they don't like me. I always go out hunting but this time they got in my way. I need to make it right. Maybe they were only scared because I am big. If I play a joke by sneaking up on him, maybe they will think I'm funny and forgive me. So I slowly creep up and shout, "Boo!" Then everyone chases me away with giant pitchforks. I just tried to be nice and now they think I am the big bad monster yet again.

Nathan Mallinson (13)
Workington Academy, Workington

THE UNUSUAL DAY

As I sat down on the couch, I noticed something running past my back window. I felt on edge so I picked up my zapper just in case. As I did so, I heard a knock on the door. I froze. Then I heard a more urgent noise. *Bang! Bang! Bang!* All of a sudden, the door broke down. A giant fish walked through the doorway and swung its flipper at me. I dodged it and hit it on the head. I then chucked it into the tank. It became very small. What on Earth was it doing here today?

Abigail Bewley (13)
Workington Academy, Workington

ZEUS THE TOE DESTROYER

I never really belonged. It all started when my dad threw me out of the house. I was seeking revenge. So, when he rested I broke into the house and went to the bottom of his bed and ripped off all ten of his toes. After that day it was never the same. I had suddenly become addicted to the taste of toe. After that night I went all around the village eating all the villagers' toes. It was all fun and games until one night. No one expected me to be a dog.

Aaron Moore (12)
Workington Academy, Workington

YoungWriters
— Est. 1991 —

YOUNG WRITERS
INFORMATION

We hope you have enjoyed reading this book – and
that you will continue to in the coming years.

If you're a young writer who enjoys reading and creative
writing, or the parent of an enthusiastic poet or story writer,
do visit our website www.youngwriters.co.uk. Here you
will find free competitions, workshops and games, as well
as recommended reads, a poetry glossary and our blog.
There's lots to keep budding writers motivated to write!

If you would like to order further copies of this book,
or any of our other titles, then please give us a
call or order via your online account.

Young Writers
Remus House
Coltsfoot Drive
Peterborough
PE2 9BF
(01733) 890066
info@youngwriters.co.uk

Join in the conversation!
Tips, news, giveaways and much more!

 YoungWritersUK 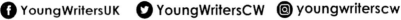 YoungWritersCW  youngwriterscw